CRYPTID CIRCUS

GERRY GRIFFITHS

SEVERED PRESS
HOBART TASMANIA

CRYPTID CIRCUS

ISBN: 978-1-922323-12-5

DEDICATION

To my lovely wife, Marilyn

1

KOKO

The van was an oven, which did nothing to improve Koko's mood as he sweltered in his costume. His stupid Afro wig itched like it was crawling with lice.

He wished idiot parents would book their kids' birthday parties in the morning, not mid-afternoon when it was ninety degrees. All he wanted was to get out of the damn heat and step under an ice-cold shower. He could feel the powder puff already clumping on his white face paint.

The catering truck moved up to the guard shack and he was next in line, so he quickly checked himself in the side mirror then squeezed on his big red sponge nose.

After a short exchange, the guard waved the caterer through.

Koko edged up and gave the guard a goofy grin. "Howdy doo, Officer!"

"Afternoon." The security guard peered inside and slowly inspected the cab. He studied Koko's face like he was counting the clown's teeth then stared at the balloon banner draped behind the two front seats blocking the view into the back.

"You got kiddies?" Koko asked, knowing he better act fast. The last thing he needed was to be subjected to a car search. Sure, if things got dicey the Walther P22 was within easy reach, tucked between the seat and the door. He shot a glance down at the pistol painted pink and black, the muzzle colored red to make it look like a kid's toy.

"Yeah, two girls," the guard replied.

"What are their ages?"

"One's five, the other one's seven."

Koko's mouth watered. "Great ages. Here, let me give you some complimentary coupons if you ever need my services at a party."

"I'm really not suppose—"

"Take them! Kids love me!"

"All right. Thanks," the guard said, palming the coupons. He used his pen and ticked off a box on a list on his clipboard. "You're clear to go. Have fun."

"Oh, I plan to," Koko said and drove onto the Rollins estate.

* * *

Margo Rollins went into the kitchen for a well-deserved break and poured herself a glass of red wine. She was careful not to spill on her chiffon blouse. Her feet were killing her from the new heels but it was important to look her best. There was so much going on with Amy turning seven, planning her birthday party, and Jonathan's campaign. The house was like Grand Central Station with all the people coming and going.

She glanced out the kitchen window. The canopies had been set up with chairs and tables for over a hundred guests. Margo's invitation list had included families so there were thirty children in attendance, even though Amy had never met most of them before, as they were the offspring of prominent parents rallying behind Jonathan in support of the senator's race in the upcoming presidential election.

Karl Truman skulked into the kitchen. "Margo. Please tell your housekeeper not to keep interrupting us when we're working. If we want something to eat, we'll ask."

"I'm sorry, Karl. I'll speak to Maria."

"Shouldn't you be out there mingling?"

"Let me remind you, that you are Jonathan's campaign manager, not mine."

"More reason for you to be out there swinging votes."

"Let me tend to my daughter. I want this to be her day."

"Fine."

"How *is* the campaign coming?"

"We're still down in the polls."

"Sounds to me, you need to strengthen my husband's platform."

"What, like a catchy slogan?"

"Jonathan is what this country needs right now."

"Margo, you and I know it. We just have to convince the rest of America."

Karl grabbed a plate of sandwiches from the counter and walked out as Caroline, Margo's seventeen-year-old daughter, entered the kitchen. Caroline waited until Karl was out of earshot before saying, "That guy is such a dick."

"Caroline!" But then Margo had to laugh. "Yeah, I guess he is but you better not let your father hear you say that."

"Why, it's true."

Margo drank her wine. She poured herself another glass and took a swallow.

She gazed out the window.

Amy's party was a success. Everyone seemed to be having a good time, as there were plenty of festivities to keep the guests amused.

A young woman dressed up as a cowgirl led a Shetland pony carrying a young boy while a short line of children waited their turn. Kids ran and played, shooting each other with water guns. A table was set up for face painting. The caterers busily served food to the guests and bussed tables. Soon it would be time for opening presents and cake.

Everything was running smoothly.

Margo was about to tip her wineglass to her lips again, when she spotted the clown she had hired standing off by his van in the parking area adjacent to the large backyard.

Caroline joined her mother at the window. "Definitely something wrong with this picture."

Smoking a cigarette, the man had removed his red fright wig and hung it on the side mirror. He was bald except for the gray hair over his ears, frizzy from sweat. The man had to be in his sixties. He looked ludicrous standing there in his clown costume.

There was something odd about him. The way he just stood there, puffing on his cigarette, and staring at the children.

"He gives me the creeps," Caroline said.

Margo couldn't agree more.

* * *

"Mrs. Rollins, come quick," Maria said in a panicked voice, standing in the doorway to the senator's library.

Jonathan looked up from behind his massive oak desk.

Karl sat forward in a high back chair. "How many times—"

"What is it, Maria?" Margo said, sliding her bare feet off the couch and sitting up. She was winding down after the hectic afternoon. All the guests had already left and the cleaning crew was just finishing up.

"I've looked everywhere!"

"Slow down, what's wrong?"

"She's not in the house."

"Check Amy's room again," Margo said. "You know how she likes to play hide-and-seek with you."

3

"No, Amy's in the kitchen. Having more cake."
Jonathan bolted to his feet. "What are you saying, Maria?"
"It's Caroline. She's gone!"

2

CARNIVAL EXTRAVAGANZA

FBI Special Agent Anna Rivers pulled up to the cyclone fence gate and let the Crown Victoria idle in park. "There's a chain and padlock."

"I'll get it," FBI Special Agent Mack Hunter said and got out on the passenger side of the car.

Anna reached down, pulled the lever, and popped the trunk.

Mack walked around to the back of the car and raised the trunk lid. After rummaging inside, he slammed the trunk shut. He strode over to the gate and effortlessly snipped the chain with a heavy-duty bolt cutter and pushed the gate open. He came back to the car, climbed in, and tossed the tool onto the backseat.

Anna threw the car into gear and proceeded through the gateway. The secluded dirt road stretched out over the flat barren landscape, the ground a slushy brown from the snowmelt. Beyond, dark looming clouds shrouded the foothills.

"That's it," Anna said. Up ahead was an abandoned industrial park with a large warehouse building.

As the sedan drew closer, the agents saw six long trailers parked in a row. Even though the wind and grit had scoured the sides of the trailers and the sun had scorched the metal, and most of the advertisement's paint had weathered off, there was still enough of the faded artwork to make out the trademark Ferris wheel and the name of the once-traveling troop *Carnival Extravaganza.*

Two big rig tractors looked like relics from a devastating world-ending war. The tires on the trucks were brittle gray and flat. Both windshields had been smashed and most of the other windows were either shattered or void of glass. Every metal part on the cabs and frames, including the rims had been rendered to rust.

Anna parked the car beside a suspicious van near the building and turned off the engine.

The agents got out of the car and drew their handguns. They approached the vehicle with a large caricature of a smiling clown holding a suspended cluster of balloons on the side panel with contact information of how to book school functions, baby showers, and birthday shows with *KoKo the Clown.*

Anna peered in the passenger window. She saw trash on the seat and floor, take-out bags and crumbled wrappers. She glanced over at the steering column. "No keys in the ignition."

Mack stepped around to the back of the van. He grabbed the handle to the rear doors. He turned the handle and slowly opened one side, aiming his gun into the interior of the van. Anna joined him and drew back the other door.

"Jesus, Anna, will you look at this?" Mack climbed inside.

Behind the two seats up front was a heavy duty mesh screen and a rolled up tarp suspended on the headliner, so that when the tarp was dropped and the back doors were closed—and mostly likely locked—any occupants would be trapped inside.

An amateurishly crafted wooden bench took up one side. Metal eyelets had been bolted to the floor with a short chain looped through to a set of ankle bracelets.

On the opposite side of the cargo area, a single-size mattress with disturbing stains, positioned on top of a narrow plank of plywood supported off the metal floor by a cinderblock foundation.

Mack noticed a produce crate filled with rolls of gray duct tape, a small burlap sack, plastic ties, pharmaceutical vials of sleeping pills and tranquilizers, bottles of chloroform and rags, and syringes in a clear sandwich bag.

Three cardboard boxes contained clown costumes and accessories: green, blue, cotton candy, orange, and red Afro wigs; giant sneakers and large multi-colored clown shoes with fat toes; baggy pants with fancy striped suspenders.

A plastic tote contained a magician's wand, an over-sized deck of cards, streamer handkerchiefs, a rubber chicken, and some foam props.

Mack spotted a red toolbox covered with cartoon animal stickers. He opened the lid and was appalled to find it stocked with various styles of knives, some of them rusted with dried blood along with pliers and a few small handsaws.

Perhaps the most disturbing were the tube-length balloons interlocked together in the shapes of different zoo animals dangling like innocent mobiles from the headliner over the makeshift bed.

"Look there," Anna said, standing by the back bumper and pointing at a woman's tan shoe sticking out from under the bed.

Mack reached down and picked it up. "It's hers."

"Think we should call for backup?" Anna asked Mack as he climbed out of the van and they walked up to the door leading into the warehouse.

"There's no time. We might already be too late."

3

GRIM DISCOVERY

Except for the scant sunlight filtering down from the high windows above the crossbeams, the rest of the warehouse's interior was ominous and cast in shadows.

"Will you look at this place?" Anna said.

Even though they each had flashlights, they chose not to use them in fear of giving away their positions.

Slowly, they weaved through a maze of defunct amusement park machinery.

They passed a broken-down Tilt-A-Wheel, the kind that spun around so fast that it would cause riders to stick to the wall by centrifugal force when the bottom fell out, a carousel with hand-carved parading steeds, and an enormous six-armed Octopus.

The agents continued on by a fortuneteller and a weight prediction booth. Next was a Swing Ride designed to rotate chairs suspended at high-speed. They came across giant teacups and bumper cars shaped like rocket ships and a few Ferris wheel gondolas. Further on were colossal billboards framed with oversized light bulbs, engines and pulley systems, and other mechanical apparatus.

Anna halted and whispered to her partner, "Mack, look over there."

Mack followed Anna through a pedestrian opening in a ten-foot tall sign—*Welcome to Carnival Extravaganza*—propped up against a bisected portion of trestle. A dim light flittered ahead. After a few more steps, they realized it was a battery-operated lantern with a dying power source poorly illuminating a small area.

"Jesus," Anna said, and aimed her gun in a two-handed grip.

Six clowns stood in a semi-circle.

"Relax, they're not real," Mack assured her.

They were life-size cardboard cutouts of Koko the Clown.

"What *is* this place?"

Ten 4-by-8 foot sheets of plywood were leaning up against the trestle. Figures dressed in women's clothes, some of them in shorts, others in dresses or shirts and pants, all of them wearing shoes or sneakers, were nailed to the boards. The arms were spread out from the bodies, the hands impaled to the wood.

Each face was completely covered with a big happy face sticker.

Mack reached up and touched one of the hands. "It's Styrofoam. They're all made of Styrofoam."

"Think it's some kind of ritual?"

"Maybe this is how he keeps score."

"Sick bastard."

"These must be the victims' clothes."

"So where are they? What does he do with them?"

"Good question. Hey, what's that smell?" Mack turned and followed his nose. He walked over to a doorway to a gaming booth labeled Water Gun Fun and ripped down the blanket nailed over the entrance.

The smell nearly bowled him over but he went in anyway. It was pitch dark in the enclosure, so Mack turned on his flashlight against his better judgment.

"Ooh that reeks. What's in here, an old portable toilet?" Anna said. She pinched her nose, stepping in after her partner.

Mack shined the beam on a large animal enclosure.

"What is that, a lion cage?" Anna said.

"Could be." Mack panned his light between the thick bars. The beam shone on a rumpled blanket, a piece of clothing, an empty water dish and a crusty food bowl, and a metal bucket with a handle.

Mack shined the light inside the bucket. "There's your answer."

Dried clumps of black feces caked the bottom of the pail.

"What kind of animal puts a human being in a cage?" Anna said.

Mack spotted another walkthrough at the far end of the booth. "Let's see where this leads."

They entered another open space with two tables. Large barrel glass jars were lined up on the tabletops. Mack shined his flashlight down and saw a billboard—*Carnival Extravaganza's Freaks and Oddities*—lying on the floor. He raised the beam on the jars and approached the tables.

"What are these things?" he said.

"They look like giant pickle jars," Anna replied.

Mack got closer and shined the light on a jar. His hip jarred the table and the thing in the jar turned in the yellowish brine. Two blue spheres peered out through kelp-like strands.

Mack jumped back.

"What is it?" Anna said.

"It's a head."

Anna walked over and peered inside the jar. She reached over, twisted off the cap, and turned the jar upside down, spilling the brine and dumping out its contents onto the floor.

"What the hell are you doing?"

"Relax, Mack. It's not real."

"What?"

Anna knelt and prodded the head with the muzzle of her gun. "See, rubber. It's fake."

"Son of a—"

They both turned when they heard the muffled cry.

"It came from over there," Anna said.

"I'll double back around!"

Anna ducked under a large mechanical arm next to the wall. She made her way along the wall and paused when she saw a sliver of light. Sunlight was filtering in through a vertical slit next to an exit door with a push bar that had been propped open with a length of pipe wedged between the bottom of the door and the doorjamb.

She opened the door and stepped outside, making sure the pipe remained in place so she would be able to come back inside. If the door closed, she would be locked out and would have to go around and come in through the other entrance.

A compound was behind the building enclosed by a cyclone fence with wooden slats inserted in the links to provide privacy.

Anna entered the storage area and found it stocked with fifty-five gallon metal drums. On one side were approximately twenty empty drums. Lids and locking rings were piled in a corner next to a mound concealed under a large blue tarp. Anna reached down and flipped up a corner of the tarp.

Underneath were evenly stacked sacks.

Anna read the label.

The sacks contained calcium oxide, commonly known as quick lime. When used, the white caustic alkaline crystalline would heat up, reaching temperatures of over fifteen hundred degrees, a process called calcination and would eventually roast any solid.

Anna saw over a dozen drums with lids. She unsnapped the locking ring of one of the drums and slipped it off. She jimmied off the lid.

She looked inside and saw a swill of organic slurry. Backing away, Anna doubled over and threw up.

After a bout of gagging and spitting up, Anna wiped her mouth and chin. She had to get back inside and tell Mack what she had found.

She dashed toward the exit door to go back inside.

But before she could reach the door, someone pulled the pipe back inside and the door banged shut.

Anna ran up and hit the door with her fist.

4

MAGIC ACT

Mack heard a door slam.

It was too dark to really tell but it sounded like it came from the rear of the warehouse. Koko was making his escape. Probably running around the side of the building to get to his van.

Mack turned and hurried back in the direction he had originally come. He dashed by the fake oddities and scurried past the diabolical cage. He stopped for a second to get his bearings.

Something metallic touched the side of his head.

Before he could react, a deafening screech blasted into his ear.

Mack dropped his gun, clamped his hand to his right ear, and crumbled to his knees. The pain was excruciating. His fingers became hot and sticky with blood.

He gazed up.

Koko the Clown stood a few feet away. His arm was around the waist of an unconscious, heavily sedated teenage girl: Caroline Rollins. Her dress was torn with dirty smudges, and she wore only one shoe.

Koko tossed an object on the floor in front of Mack.

It was an air horn.

Bastard had blown out his eardrum.

"Caroline?" Mack said.

The girl was too drugged up to respond.

Koko reached inside his jumbo pants.

Mack searched frantically for his gun.

Koko the Clown sneered and pulled out a pink and black toy gun with a red muzzle.

This is a joke, right? Mack thought to himself.

Koko aimed.

So what, one of those silly banners is going to stick out of the barrel saying BANG!

A real gunshot echoed in the cavernous warehouse.

* * *

Even though Anna held three marksman badges from the gun range she still hesitated whether to take the shot, afraid she might hit the Rollins girl but knew if she didn't, Mack would be dead for sure.

The bullet grazed Koko in the shoulder. He jerked back, releasing the young woman who collapsed on the floor.

"Step away from the girl!" Mack had retrieved his gun and was pointing it at the clown.

Koko didn't move. The red face paint around his lips was so exaggerated that when he grinned, his yellow teeth made his mouth look hideous.

"You heard him! Back off!" Anna aimed her gun and marched toward the kidnapper.

"As you wish." With a quick sleight of hand, Koko flung a tiny ball on the floor and a blinding cloud of smoke erupted between him and Anna.

Koko was gone in the few split seconds it took for the smoke to clear.

"Mack, stay with the girl." Anna dashed into the menagerie of decrepit amusement attractions, weaving through the relics. She heard a door opening and slamming and followed the sounds.

Throwing open the door, Anna stepped outside. She panned her gun from side to side. She realized she had exited from a different door from where they had originally entered the building.

An engine started around the corner and tires churned up the ground.

Anna raced around the edge of the building and she saw the van speeding away. She glanced over at the Crown Victoria.

All four tires had been flattened.

"Shit."

5

MACK'S CRAZY IDEA

A week later Mack and Anna visited the Rollins's estate to see how Caroline was adjusting after her frightening ordeal. Once inside, they were directed to the library and found Jonathan Rollins and Karl Truman in a heated debate.

"Enough about demographics, Karl. If I'm to have any chance of winning, I need to capture the middle-class vote, not just the Asian and Hispanic. I need to get the message to all American families. I want to be a president remembered for protecting the children of our future."

"Do you think Bush will be remembered for passing the No Child Left Behind Act, or Obama, The Children's Health Insurance Program? No, because they were overshadowed by that damn war."

"But that doesn't mean—" Jonathan paused when he saw Mack and Anna standing in the doorway. "Oh, don't mind us. Please, do come in."

Mack and Anna entered and sat in two chairs facing the center of the room. Margo, Caroline, and Amy were lounging on the couch. Caroline was snuggling with her mother.

"How is your ear?" Jonathan asked Mack.

"Doctor says I may experience some hearing loss on the one side but it will eventually heal."

"You were lucky your partner came back when she did."

"That I am," Mack said and gave Anna a nod.

"The man, who abducted my daughter, do you have any idea who he is?"

"His name is John Paul Elroy," Mack said. "He performed as Koko the Clown for Carnival Extravaganza for twenty years before the company went belly up. That's what led us to the warehouse."

"Seems during that time, the circus traveled all over the U.S., small towns mostly before they became a thing of the past," Anna said. "We suspect he was abducting young women from every town and kept it up after he started his own business."

"My Lord," Jonathan said. "How do we protect our children from such monsters?"

"Short of putting microchips into each kid?" Mack quipped.

"Surely, you're not suggesting..." Jonathan paused.

Mack shrugged his shoulders. "Hey, we love our pets enough to give them microchips to identify them, why not put tracking chips in the children."

"I have to say, it is an intriguing concept," Jonathan said. "Maybe something to consider for the campaign. What do you think, Karl?"

"I think it's absurd," Karl grunted. "Sounds like something out of a George Orwell novel."

"Not if you consider there are as many as 100,000 active missing persons cases a year in the U.S. alone," Mack piped in. "Think if all those people had a microchip tracking device implanted in them, they would all be home, safe and sound right now." Mack looked over and saw Anna giving him a strange look like he had lost his mind.

"It's radical, I'll give it that, but it would put an end to child abductions, now wouldn't it," Jonathan said.

"No parent would ever go for it," Karl said. "It's too controversial."

"Of course, rights to privacy would be an issue," Jonathan said, "but once a person reached a certain age, the implant could be removed if they desired."

Amy looked up at her mother. "Mommy, does that mean I have to get a shot?"

"No stupid," Caroline said.

"Well, I don't know, maybe," Margo said, looking at Jonathan who was mulling over the idea. She glanced down at Amy. "But it would be a good shot."

"Looks like we have much to discuss," Jonathan said.

"Well, if you'll excuse us," Mack said, getting up from his chair.

Anna stood and gave Caroline, Amy, and Mrs. Rollins a warm smile. "You take care."

Mrs. Rollins glanced up at Anna. "Promise me, you'll catch the son of a bitch."

"We promise," Anna replied and left the room with Mack.

On their way to the car, Anna turned to Mack. "Were you really serious back there? Microchips?"

"Sure, why not," he said with a sly grin. He turned serious for a moment. "You do know what happens when an FBI agent makes a promise like you did to Mrs. Rollins?"

"Yeah," Anna said. "They damn well better keep it."

6

CURBSIDE PICKUP

Suzie Fryer's heart fluttered the moment the engine choked and stalled. She cranked the steering wheel and coasted onto the shoulder of the road.

"What's going on?" Cindy Jacobs gasped from the front passenger seat.

"We're out of gas."

"Didn't you check the gas gauge?"

"Doesn't work. My dad says there's something wrong with the floaty-thingy in the tank."

"Now what?" Cindy said, glancing out the passenger window at the pitch-dark night.

Suzie stared out the windshield at the short expanse of road lit up by the headlights. She hit the high beams. Just more desolate road and flat desert. She killed the lights not wanting to run down the battery. Running out of gas was bad enough. Her dad would throw a fit if he had to pour more money into Suzie's beater replacing the battery. "Think if you call your mom she'd come and get us?"

"Suzie, it's almost midnight. I'm supposed to be grounded, remember? I had to sneak out. Besides, my mom has my phone. Part of my punishment."

"Well, I can't call my dad, he's at work."

"So what are we going to do?"

"Looks like we walk."

"Suzie, it's over two miles back to town."

"I know, but what choice do we have." Suzie reached across and opened the glove compartment. She grabbed the flashlight, flicked the switch but the bulb didn't light up. She slapped the housing in the palm of her hand and the flashlight came on. She handed the flashlight to Cindy hoping it would ease her friend's unease being stranded so far from home in the middle of the night.

Suzie opened her door and was halfway out when she looked back inside. "Make sure you lock your side."

"Really, you think someone's going to want to steal this piece of—"

"Maybe I should hold the flashlight."

Cindy got out, slapped the door lock knob, and shoved the door closed with her hip.

Suzie slid out and locked her side. Not that there was much inside worth stealing. She doubted if anyone would be interested in her book bag on the floor behind the front seat or Johnny Miles' letterman jacket he'd left in her backseat.

Zipping up her sweatshirt, Suzie saw Cindy doing the same. It had been a typical sweltering New Mexico day hitting the mid-nineties but had cooled down considerably for the night. Suzie shuddered to shake off the chill.

They started down the side of the road.

Suzie doubted very seriously if they would see anyone driving by at this time of night. If they did, it would probably be a drunk with no business being behind the wheel and would be the last person they would want to get in a car with. Better to be safe than sorry and say no thanks if such a person stopped and offered them a ride.

And she certainly didn't want for them to get hit walking on the side of the road and end up in some ditch left to die while the hit-and-run driver sped away with no recollection the following day of how the front of his car got mangled with blood on the grill.

Suzie heard the faint air horn of a Santa Fe passing in the distance.

After walking for almost half an hour, Suzie heard a car engine approaching behind them. She turned and saw headlights coming down the road. She turned to Cindy. "Hey, we're in luck. Maybe we can get a ride." She stood on the edge of the road and waved her hand to flag down the driver.

As it got closer, Suzie saw that it was a van.

Fifty feet away, the vehicle lurched to a stop. The headlights flicked to high beams, blinding Suzie and Cindy.

"What's he doing?" Cindy said, stepping behind Suzie.

"I don't know. Either he's debating whether to pick us up or he's being a jerk."

They waited while the engine continued to idle.

Suddenly, the headlights went out, pitching the girls into darkness.

"I don't like this," Cindy said, unable to conceal the panic in her voice.

Suzie could hear the van's tires turning slowly over the asphalt—like a predator creeping up on its prey. "Get ready to run."

"Where? It's pitch black out here."

"Give me your hand." Suzie felt Cindy's sweaty palm. Her friend was shaking.

The van was only twenty feet away.

Suzie still couldn't see the driver, or if there was anyone sitting in the front passenger seat. She wondered if there might be more of them lurking in the back cargo area, part of a human trafficking ring waiting to nab two unsuspecting girls, stupid enough to be wandering way out in the middle of nowhere in the dead of night.

She tensed her muscles, ready to make a mad dash for it just as the van's headlights came back on like a pair of glaring halogen spotlights. The engine roared and the van raced toward them, veering so the centerline of the bumper hugged the edge where the tarmac lane met the shoulder of the road.

Suzie pushed Cindy and they dove onto the dirt.

The van narrowly missed them, cut back onto the asphalt, and thundered off.

"Jesus, Suzie, that maniac almost ran us over." Cindy got up, holding her arm.

"Asshole!" Suzie yelled when she was on her feet. She looked at her friend. "Are you okay?"

"Yeah, I just scraped my elbow."

They waited until the sound of the engine faded away.

"Come on," Suzie said. "He's gone."

They continued on but hadn't gone more than half a mile when Cindy grabbed Suzie's arm. "Did you hear that?"

"Hear what?"

"There's something out there."

"I didn't hear anything. You're just paranoid after that jerk in the van."

"No, I definitely heard a noise."

Suzie glanced around but it was difficult to see much in the dark. Normally, this time of night the sky would be jewel studded with thousands of stars and moonlight, but tonight the tapestry above was obscured by gray low-hanging clouds, the tail end of a passing storm front.

The rocky desert around them was somewhat flat with sagebrush and granite hillocks—a natural hunting ground for large predators.

Suzie took a moment and listened for any telltale sounds. She heard what might have been an owl or a hawk swoop down maybe twenty feet away into a bush, followed by a petrified squeak as the bird of prey soared off. She was about to tell Cindy that there was nothing to worry about when she heard the parade of footfalls to her right.

"See, I told you I wasn't making it up," Cindy said, shining the dim flashlight.

Suzie turned and saw a small band of coyotes—maybe five or six—trotting in the shadows.

"Cindy, pick up the pace." Suzie nudged her friend and they broke into a slow jog. She knew they couldn't outrun the pack but it was important to stay ahead of the wild canines, as they liked to attack head-on, unlike wolves that chose to chase down their prey. She knew coyotes normally shied away from humans but these animals seemed intent on following them.

"Are they still coming?" Cindy asked, too afraid to look back.

"Yep." Knowing they would soon grow tired from running, Suzie halted dead in her tracks and faced the stalking pack. She raised her hands above her head and shouted, "Get away! Go! Get!"

Cindy stopped and turned.

Suzie stared at Cindy. "Don't just stand there! Yell!"

Cindy waved her arms and hollered, "Go! Leave us alone!"

Suzie spotted a rock and picked it up. She hurled it at the pack. A coyote yelped and the group backed away. She found another rock and threw it. Another coyote cried out. She could hear the pack retreat into the darkness.

"My God, Suzie are you crazy?"

"Hey, I read if you're ever confronted by a mountain lion, make a lot of noise and wave your hands. I figured if it works for a big cat it should work for this bunch."

"Thank God you were right."

"Let's keep moving."

Fifteen minutes later, they were standing on a rise looking down at the gloomy town below.

Cindy shined the beam of the flashlight on Buckhorn's town sign, pop. 3512, peppered with 22-caliber bullet holes.

Instead of a string of businesses nestled together on a main street, Buckhorn was a scattering of establishments separated on flat parcels of hard packed clay and siltstone, surrounded by barrel cactus, Mohave prickly pear, and saguaro with upraised arms giving the appearance of surrendering soldiers.

Apparently, the city council saw no rhyme or reason to the layout of the town, almost as though a toddler had thrown down a set of building blocks to lie where they may.

The gated community outside of town looked like a fortress in the distance surrounded by a perimeter of ten-foot tall stucco walls.

Hurrying down to the first building—a two-pump Texaco with a lube bay—Suzie grabbed Cindy suddenly and pulled her behind the dumpster by the side of the building.

"What are—?"

"Quiet," Suzie whispered.

A set of headlights came down the road.

"Why are we hiding?"

"That's why." Suzie made sure Cindy caught a good glimpse of the passing vehicle. Sheriff Joseph Gooding was behind the wheel on a nightly patrol.

Suzie waited until the sheriff's cruiser turned down another street before saying, "I don't think he'd be too keen on us roaming around. Think if he brought us home."

"My mom would lock me in my room and throw away the key," Cindy said.

"Come on, before he comes back." Suzie led the way. They kept to the shadows as much as possible, racing past a few trailers and houses, running behind the BBQ & GRILL, and down a side street where they stopped at an intersection.

"You can keep the flashlight. Give it to me later," Suzie said.

"What are you going to do about your car?"

"My dad won't be off his shift for another six hours. I'll call Johnny before school starts and have him run me back with some gas. No one will ever know."

"Let's hope not. See you in class." Cindy dashed off and quickly disappeared in the dark.

Suzie headed in the direction of her house. If she was lucky, she might be able to get four or five hours sleep before she would have to get up and get ready for school.

Her dad kept a couple of one-gallon gas cans in the garage she could use to fill up at the station after Johnny picked her up. She hoped he didn't make a stink about helping her out. He'd been acting strange lately, hinting that he wanted his jacket back.

Her home was a block away.

Dust covered most of the cars and trucks parked on the street.

Almost to her house, she noticed a van parked at the curb but facing the wrong direction—the same van from earlier.

The cab was dark. She didn't remember ever seeing the vehicle in town before and wondered if whoever had been driving it had stolen the vehicle and abandoned the van. Even though it was covered in a thick layer of dust, she could still see images painted on the front grill and driver side door.

Are those balloons?

Suzie was surprised to see the side sliding door on the van had been left open. She paused to look inside.

A white-gloved hand reached out of the gloom and yanked her inside. The last thing she remembered was the door slamming shut then a stabbing pain in her neck and her world going dark.

7

MISSING PERSONS

Sheriff Joseph Gooding stepped out of his office and escorted Camden Fryer to the front desk. He gave the grieving man a pat on the back. "I'm sorry I don't have more to tell you, Camden. I know this hasn't been easy but I want you to know we're doing everything in our power to find Suzie."

"This isn't like her. Running off," Camden said, choking back the tears. "Sure, I know I'm hard on her but it isn't easy, a father raising a daughter all on his own."

"No, I'm sure it's not." Joseph paused and tapped on the counter to get his deputy's attention.

Shelly looked up from her computer, fingers hovering over the keyboard. She took one look at Camden's glum face. "Don't worry, we'll find her."

"I sure hope so."

Joseph held up a folder. "Shelly, could you log this report into the system?"

"Toss it in the bin."

Joseph placed the folder in the near-empty in-box on the corner of her desk.

Shelly gave Camden a warm smile and went back to tapping on the keyboard.

As soon as Camden was gone, Joseph sighed and leaned back against the counter. "Poor guy's worried sick."

Shelley stopped typing. "Can you blame him? It's been 36 hours."

"I know, but I don't know what more we can do. Search parties found nothing, we notified the State Troopers, dispatched a statewide APB, and still no sign of her. Any word from the FBI?"

"Not a peep."

"Well, I guess we're just going to—" Joseph turned when he heard the front door push open and two people stepped inside. The man looked to be in his mid-thirties, wearing black slacks and black dress shoes, and a white long-sleeved shirt, cuffs rolled up mid-forearm, the top button undone, no tie. The woman maybe a couple years younger, attractive, black pantsuit and white blouse, and black flats. Glocks holstered on their hips.

The woman held up her identification. "I'm Special FBI Agent Anna Rivers and this is Special FBI Agent Mack Hunter. We're with the MPD—Missing Persons Division."

"You're here about Suzie Fryer?" Joseph asked.

"That's right."

"Thank God," Shelly blurted.

"Thank you for coming." Joseph shook their hands while Shelly got up from her desk and came out from behind the counter. "This is my wife, Shelly. Shelly runs the office. She's also my deputy."

"Husband and wife team, I like that," Anna said, shaking Shelly's hand.

"What do they say 'behind every good man there's a good woman watching his back,'" Mack grinned.

"You should know," Anna said.

"Please, come into my office." Joseph motioned to the open door.

"Would you care for some coffee or a cold drink?" Shelly asked.

"Coffee would be super," Anna replied.

Mack ran his fingers through his thick damp hair. "A bottled water would be nice."

Joseph pulled another chair into his office and placed it beside the chair facing the front of his desk to accommodate the agents. He waited until Shelly came in with the drinks and everyone got settled before sitting behind his desk. Shelly sat on the edge of the credenza by the wall.

Anna and Mack took their Smart phones out of their pants pockets. Anna gazed down at hers then looked up at Joseph and Shelly. "Sorry, we're not being rude. We have the report you sent the Bureau on our phones. This way we can follow along and add notes. So Sheriff, if you want to run us through it."

"Sure. Two nights ago, sometime around midnight, Suzie Fryer's car ran out of gas approximately two miles east out of town, which is where we found it. We know this because we have a statement from her friend, Cindy Jacobs, who was with her at the time and got worried when Suzie didn't show up for school. When Cindy couldn't reach Suzie on her cell phone and the girl was nowhere to be found, Cindy reluctantly came into our office."

"You said reluctantly," Anna said. "Why?"

"Cindy wasn't even supposed to be out. She'd been grounded by her mother."

"I see. Go on."

"As Suzie's father was working the graveyard shift and Cindy's mom had forbidden her from going out, both girls couldn't call their parents and decided to walk home."

"Two miles in the dark, after midnight?" Mack inquired.

"That's right," Joseph replied.

"How would you describe Buckhorn?"

"Pretty dull," Joseph said. "There's the tavern just out of town but I wouldn't exactly call it lively."

Shelly curled her fingers over the lip of the credenza and leaned forward. "Most folks turn in early around here. Roll up the sidewalks, you might say, those that have them. Buckhorn's what you might call one of those little sleepy border towns." She looked over at Joseph. "When was the last time we had a guest?"

"Ah, that would have been Kenny Thompson for drunk and disorderly," Joseph said thinking back. "That had to have been two, no, three weeks ago."

"I remember," Shelly said. "He threw up all over the cell."

"I told you I would have cleaned it up."

"Getting back to the girls," Mack glanced at the screen on his cell phone. "It doesn't specify here, but how long were the girls together?" Mack asked the sheriff.

"Cindy said they were almost home. Maybe a couple of blocks away when they spilt up."

"And to the best of your knowledge, Suzie never made it back to her house?"

"We don't believe so. Her father said he never saw her again after he came home from his shift."

"Do you have any reason to suspect the father of foul play?" Anna asked.

"No," Shelly burst in. "Absolutely not. They may have been having problems but Camden adores his daughter."

"Problems how?" Mack asked.

"Camden hasn't been the same after his wife passed a year ago from leukemia. He took it pretty hard."

"Sorry to hear that," Anna said. "What does Mr. Fryer do for a living?"

"He's a security guard at the Desert Sands Estates," Joseph told her. "I understand he puts in a lot of hours."

"So he's absent a lot," Mack concluded, "leaving Suzie alone to do whatever she wants."

"Whoa," Shelly piped in. "I know Suzie. She's a good kid. Whatever happened, I doubt she ran off."

"That's what I'm thinking, too," Joseph said. "If Suzie was going to leave town, why go without her car? She could have gotten someone to help her gas it up."

"I totally agree," Anna said, glancing at the small screen on her phone. "Tell us about the van."

Joseph sat back in his swivel chair. "Cindy said that when Suzie and she were walking home this van began to stalk them. Even tried to run them over before it drove off. She did notice a large crack in the windshield on the passenger side and an oval decal sticker with the letters **NM**."

"That's not going to be much help," Shelly said. "Just about every vehicle in the state has that sticker plastered somewhere on their car."

"Had she ever seen this van before?" Anna asked.

"No."

"What about the driver?"

"No, she couldn't see who was behind the wheel. Only a brief description of the vehicle; old white Ford Econoline van with a worn paintjob."

"Which is why we're here," Mack said. "After reading your report you sent us, it got us thinking about a past case we had when a teenage girl was abducted."

"Did you solve the case?" Shelly asked.

"We rescued the victim. But we were never able to apprehend the suspect."

"And you think this could be the same person?"

"Possibly," Anna said. "We ran the information you gave us into our data file and ran an algorithm that told us we might have a pattern."

"What kind of pattern?" Joseph asked.

"That our guy likes to abduct his victims from small rural towns."

8

SALES PITCH

Tobias Morgan tightened the last bolt and stepped back from the open compartment on the tractor's engine. He grabbed a shop rag from the workbench and wiped his hands.

He climbed up the side of the tractor onto the seat behind the large steering wheel, leaned forward, and turned the key. The engine began to crank over, giving the impression that at any moment it would roar to life, but instead the pistons clanked inside the valves and the carburetor sputtered and the motor stopped dead with a shuddering thud.

"Damn it," Tobias cursed and gave the housing plate under the steering wheel a fierce kick which sent a jarring pain up his big toe when it slammed the inside of his steel-toed boot. He slid down from the tractor, hopping on one foot and heard a vehicle pulling up outside.

He hobbled over to the open barn door.

A vintage red Cadillac convertible drove down the gravel driveway with the top down. The sun glinting off the chrome bumper blinded Tobias for a moment as the beast grinded to a stop and the driver silenced the throaty engine.

The driver's door swung open.

Out stepped a tall, lanky man with a top hat, wearing a crimson tailcoat with black lapels, tight brown trousers tucked inside black shin-high boots. He looked dressed for a fox hunt. He had a hawkish nose and thin stork like legs. He gave Tobias a big grin and marched over. "Hi there, friend."

"I don't know what you're selling but I'd appreciate if you'd get off my property." Tobias figured it was best to nip it in the bud right off the bat and not have to listen to some long drawn-out spiel about something he had no need for that he would be paying for in monthly installments for the rest of his life.

"Actually, I'm not a salesman."

"Then what are you?"

"I'm a scouting agent. I have a proposition for you."

"That so."

"I would like your permission to use a portion of your land."

Tobias studied the man for a moment. "Yeah? What, you want to lease a parcel?"

"Not exactly."

"What then? I don't want squatters camping on my land."

"No, nothing like that. We would only be here for a week maybe less and then we would be gone. You wouldn't even know we were here."

"We? There're more of you?"

"Oh, yes. I'm sorry. I haven't introduced myself. I'm J.J. Nightsinger. And you are, sir?"

"Tobias Morgan."

Nightsinger extended his long thin fingers for a handshake.

Tobias wiped his hand on his overalls and shook. "So what kind of money are we talking? To use my property," Tobias asked.

"Well, it all depends."

"On what?"

"On how many people come to see us. You would receive 5 percent of all ticket sales."

"Ticket sales, for what? Don't tell me this is some kind of carnival?"

"No, much better."

"So you're not one of those carnies?"

"Actually, we like to be called cirkies. We wear many hats. Besides my other duties I'm also the ringmaster of the circus."

"Circus! Hell no. I don't want elephants tearing up my land and shitting all over the place."

"You needn't worry. We don't have elephants."

"No?"

"They're no longer allowed. The animal rights groups stepped in to save the elephants from abuse and when the pachyderms were freed, ticket sales went into the crapper putting circuses out of business."

"And you weren't affected?"

"You might say we operate differently. If you want to hear more, we could go inside. Maybe I could get a cold beverage?"

Tobias was on the fence and wasn't sure if he wanted to sit down and give the man a listen but then he could use the money. Might even make enough to get his tractor running. Hell, if he played his cards right, and asked for a bigger percentage of the ticket sales, he might even be able to buy himself a newer used tractor.

"I do think once you hear what I have to say, you'll be quite excited," Nightsinger said, palms up and giving Tobias a beaming 'what do you have to lose' look.

"All right," Tobias said, caving in. "I guess I could hear you out. Come on in. I got a pitcher of lemonade in the fridge."

"Sounds splendid. Believe me, you won't be sorry," Nightsinger said, and followed Tobias up the porch steps and into his house.

9

THE CARAVAN

Tobias stood on his porch and watched the long caravan of vehicles coming down the road. He opened his pocket watch and checked the time. They were right on schedule like Nightsinger had promised.

Three big rig semis with fifty-five-foot long trailers and a long flatbed truck carrying the stored tents and framework, rumbled onto the flat dirt ten-acre parcel next to his field of triticale, a hybrid of wheat and rye growing near the large irrigation pond.

Each truck was painted with white and red stripes like the big top tents on the sides of the trailers with the giant bold letters—CRYPTID CIRCUS.

Tobias had heard of Ringling Brothers and Barnum & Bailey but knew nothing about what Nightsinger called "The Most Amazing Circus in the World." When Tobias tried pressuring the man for specifics, Nightsinger waved him off and said he would have to wait and see like everyone else that came to see the show.

A procession of recreation vehicles and motor homes passed through. Tobias figured they were the living quarters on wheels for the performers and the crew that worked in the circus.

Tobias noticed the artwork on the side of a Winnebago. A figure wearing a hood, poised with a throwing knife stood in front of a woman tied spread-eagled to a spinning wheel: MAGNUS THE MAGNIFICENT.

A campervan displayed a caricature drawing on the side panel of a contortionist who had shaped himself into a human pretzel and was called: ROLLO THE RUBBERMAN.

The caravan continued on and went beyond the other parked trucks. The RVs and campers split off and began to circle around, forming separate campsites like a band of gypsies.

J.J. Nightsinger rambled by in his flashy Cadillac. He tipped his hat at Tobias.

Tobias waved back and smiled at the exotic Filipino woman sitting up front with Nightsinger. She wore a flat hat with a silver bird of paradise on the top rimmed with strands of white pearls and a long veil draped down the shoulders of her gold tunic. She flipped open a fan and covered the lower part of her face.

Tobias went down the porch steps and walked to the edge of the road as another fleet of trucks entered, European models with flat fronts and high cabs. Heavy tarps covered the cargo holds.

He hoped to steal a glimpse of what was inside but the canvas covers were anchored tight to the grommets on the truck beds. Even still, it wasn't enough to contain the pungent animal smells as the trucks passed.

A truck hit a rut in the road and the back tires bounced, jolting the rig.

Tobias heard a chorus of angry roars within the concealed cargo hold. It startled him so much he took a step back. The loud truck engines quickly dampened the fierce bellowing growls.

He watched the last truck come onto his property and park with the others.

Airbrakes hissed and the engines shut down.

He counted almost thirty vehicles on his land beyond the barn. This was totally crazy. He couldn't believe he had actually agreed to do this.

Tobias Morgan was hosting a circus.

10

FUMES

Suzie found it near impossible to breathe inside the burlap hood. She kept inhaling fibers up her nose. The coarse material scratched her face, making her sweat and itch. Her parched throat felt raw. The ball gag shoved in her mouth tasted foul and hurt her tongue. Her jaw and cheek muscles ached.

Her left wrist was fastened by a plastic tie to an eyebolt by her waist while her right hand was extended over her head, bound to the inside wall of the van. Both ankles were hobbled with a tight-fitting shank of rope.

She was dying of thirst and wondered when he was going to give her some more water.

What had it been, three, four hours since her last drink?

Sitting in this hotbox. Last time, he had reached up inside the hood, yanked the ball gag out of her mouth, and shoved the end of a straw between her lips. She had managed two long pulls before he yanked the straw away and shoved the ball gag back into her mouth.

She'd lost all sense of time since her abduction. She vaguely remembered being grabbed. Her head felt like it was filled with cotton. The spot where he'd jabbed the needle into her neck still stung a little.

She wanted to scream at him, scratch his eyes out. But then she was too petrified of what he might do to her if she resisted and put up a fight. She'd felt him press against her when he was restraining her but so far he hadn't tried to grope her or force himself on her.

Which didn't make it any less creepy.

Her butt was numb from sitting on an old mattress. She could feel the ends of the coiled springs poking into her jeans.

Suzie rested the back of her head against the metal wall.

She wished she could fall asleep and wake up in her own bed and find this was all a bad nightmare.

She banged her head against the hard metal.

She was about to scream in frustration when she realized the hood had snagged on a rough edge or an exposed screw. It was enough that she could lower her head and lean forward, allowing her to see past her chest and onto her lap. If she cocked her head just right, she could...

A rear door banged open.

She tilted her head, hoping to get a look at her abductor but the backdrop of bright sunlight silhouetted the dark figure.

Suzie watched him reach inside the van and take out a box.

The door slammed closed.

Suzie heard a hissing sound and took a deep whiff.

She could smell fumes.

Gasoline!

Her heart pounded in her chest.

Oh my God, he's going to torch the van with me inside!

11

EARL SHIBE

John Paul Elroy stood on the ridge and gazed down at the farmland with the large gathering of parked vehicles that looked like a giant truck stop. He had been dogging the circus caravan for a week, wondering where it would end up. Now that they were here, he figured it would take the riggers and roustabouts a day and night to set up the tents and concession stands, a day for the artists to rehearse, and then the big opening night.

He thought about auditioning for the gaffer, impress the circus manager with some of his gags and get signed on with the other zanies but he knew it would be too risky. It pained him to have to say goodbye to his alter ego, Koko the Clown, but he had to with the FBI breathing down his neck.

His new act would be even better; Jocko the Hobo Clown. It would be the perfect disguise for what he had planned. After operating for a week, the gaffer's safe would be filled with cash. Who less to suspect walking around than a clown everyone thought was part of the show.

He walked over to where he had set up camp. Nothing elaborate; a folding chair facing a ring of rocks for a campfire, small table with a propane cook stove, a crate on the ground with cooking utensils, canned goods, and a 24-pack of Schlitz beer in a cooler.

The van was parked under the shade in a small grove of burr oaks. He walked over and paused at the driver's door. He studied his reflection in the side mirror. He saw an old man with puffy eyes and pockmarked cheeks, balding with wiry side patches of gray hair, a turkey neck, and a Lucky Strike dangling out of the corner of his mouth. It was times like this he wished he could wear his white face paint every day. Transform himself into that insanely funny clown that stalked young women.

Elroy gazed through the window at his makeup kit on the passenger seat. The lid was up displaying the tubes of face paint and small cans of powder puff, application brushes, red rubber noses, and a green fright wig. A new costume—still in the package and never worn—tucked between the kit and the backrest.

He went around to the back of the van. A red five-gallon gas can sat on the ground by the rear bumper. He removed the cap. The underside of the cap had an attached spout. He replaced the cap on the can with the spout sticking out.

He unscrewed the cap on the side of the van, grabbed the gas can, and began pouring fuel into the tank. He took a drag and blew smoke out the side of his mouth, his eyes watering slightly from the gas fumes.

The tip of his cigarette flared.

"Shit!" He spat out his cigarette and squashed the butt with the heel of his boot.

Once the gas can was drained, he placed it on the ground next to the rear tire.

Elroy opened the van's left rear door. He reached in and grabbed a cardboard box filled with aerosol paint cans. He placed the box on the ground next to the empty gas can then shut the door.

He took a spray can and removed the cap. He gave the can a vigorous shake and began spraying over the white rear doors with blue paint.

He wondered what Earl Shibe—King of the $99.95 auto paintjob—would think of his work if he were still alive. Not that he gave two shits.

12

HALF-PINT AND PENNY

Tobias had never met a little person before, let alone two.

The fellow had a big forehead and a wild shock of yellow hair. His face was painted white. Black mascara circled his eyes. He had two black heart shapes on each cheek. His nose was red and he had an exaggerated amount of red paint etched around his mouth with the corners raised in a big constant grin. He wore a snug one-piece jumpsuit with an orange and blue design, the legs red with blue stripes along with a pair of white high-top shoes.

He was slightly taller than a yardstick.

"They call me Half-Pint," the little man said, sounding like a munchkin on the Wizard of Oz. "And this is my wife, Penny."

Penny was about the same height. She was attractive in the face with a large ribbon tied on the top of her blond hair. Her face was white with blue hearts drawn around her thick eyelashes; nose red like her husband's. Her mouth was a lush pink.

She'd drawn a stitch down her forehead, nose, and mouth to her chin so that it looked like both sides of her face had been sewn together.

Like her husband, her pudgy hands extended only to her waist. She wore a yellow and blue dress, green tights over her short legs, and a tiny pair of purple pumps.

Tobias thought for a small thing, she sure was buxom.

"Pleased to meet you. I'm Tobias Morgan." Tobias put out his hand to shake.

Half-Pint shook with his child-sized hand.

Tobias was shocked by his strong grip.

"Nice to meet you," Penny said. Her voice was high-pitched like she had just spoken after inhaling from a helium-filled balloon.

He found Penny's chubby fingers calloused to the touch.

"I never met midgets before," Tobias said.

Half-Pint laughed then furrowed his brow. "First of all pal, we're not midgets. We're dwarfs."

"What, like in Snow White?"

"That's right. Got any more smart-alecky cracks?"

"Uh, no."

"Good. Just be thankful Nightsinger's letting us show you around. Normally, he doesn't do that."

"Why's that?"

"He doesn't want to jinx the show. Kind of like harmonicas."

"I play harmonica," Tobias boasted. "I do a pretty good 'Tennessee Waltz' if I do say so myself."

"Not while we're here, you won't."

"Why's that?" Tobias asked.

"Cirkies consider it bad luck. I suggest you keep it put away until we're gone."

That last thing Tobias wanted to do was to get on the wrong side of Nightsinger or any of the circus folks and jeopardize his share of the ticket sales. "To tell you the truth, I never much cared for the instrument. Get dizzy every time I play it."

"Good to hear," Half-Pint said with a grin. "Follow us and stay close."

As they walked, Half-Pint gave Tobias a crash course lesson on circus lingo so he would better understand what was going on.

A dozen roustabouts busily removed a rolled-up tent from the flatbed truck and the associated hardware. Once the canvas was on the ground, the truck rolled away and stopped where the lot man was standing. He was the supervisor in charge of the three tent locations. Everyone worked methodically, each with a specific duty. The men began rolling out the canvas until it was flat on the ground in preparation of being hoisted in the air.

"Let's park it here for a bit," Half-Pint said. He helped Penny onto an offloaded crate. He climbed up. They sat drumming their heels on the wood panel while Tobias leaned on the side of the crate, observing the seasoned veterans performing their jobs.

They watched for half an hour while the tent master worked with the riggers running the guy wires, and a small crew raised the trestles, which would be the center supports for the tent.

Three-man sledge gangs pounded large wooden stakes into the ground with heavy sledgehammers, each man taking a turn in perfect three-point harmony. The pulverized crown of each stake looked like the end of an exploding cigar.

Half-Pint jumped down from the crate. He held up his hands for Penny. She slipped down off the edge. He caught her in his arms and lowered her slowly to the ground. He looked up at Tobias. "Come, we'll introduce you around."

Half-Pint and Penny held hands and skipped together as Tobias tagged along. From the back, they looked like a cute pair of little kids, clowning around.

13

MAGNUS & LADY MCBETH

Tobias thought he had stepped onto a biker movie set when he saw Magnus the Magnificent in a black sleeveless vest, black skintight leather pants, and black combat boots. Tobias counted over a dozen throwing knives sheathed in the belt around the man's waist.

Lady McBeth, Magnus' lovely assistant, wore a black leather brazier and skintight shorts, thigh-high high-heeled boots. She looked like a seductive dominatrix casting for a porno film.

Tobias could imagine them as superheroes in a Marvel comic book.

They had already set up their props by their motor home and were in the middle of rehearsing their act when Half-Pint and Penny brought Tobias over.

"Magnus, say hi to Tobias Morgan," Half-Pint said. "This is his property."

"How do you do," Magnus said but didn't offer his hand. Instead, he stared over Tobias' shoulder as though someone was behind him. Tobias glanced back but there was no one there.

Tobias was anxious to be introduced to Lady McBeth but her attention was on Penny.

"Are those new shoes?"

"You like them?" Penny beamed with a big grin.

"They're adorable," Lady McBeth said. "Can I borrow them sometime?"

"Sure can," the munchkin replied.

Tobias thought that was a hoot. There was no way Lady McBeth's feet could fit in those tiny shoes. Then it dawned on him she was just being nice. He figured circus people were just one big happy family.

"Would Mr. Morgan care to take a ride on the Spinning Wheel of Death?" Magnus asked.

"Would I what?"

"He wants you to get on that," Half-Pint said, pointing at a red, round sheet of plywood mounted on a spindle.

"What for?"

"Perhaps you could be my new assistant," Magnus grinned, looking in Tobias' direction.

"And what is wrong with your old one," Lady McBeth said indignantly.

Tobias could tell by her smirk that it was all just part of the act.

"Well?" Magnus continued to stare at the top of Tobias' head.

"I don't think so."

"Very well. Lady McBeth?"

"I would love to, Magnus." The leather-clad assistant went over to the spinning wheel. She stepped onto the footplate with her back against the wood. She held onto the short posts on each side of her hips and rested her head between the short posts on either side of her face.

"Are you ready?" Magnus asked.

"Yes, I am ready. Mr. Morgan would you kindly spin the wheel?"

Tobias grabbed the edge and yanked down. A loud click sounded as the wheel made its first revolution. "Faster!" Lady McBeth shouted.

As the footplate came around, Tobias grabbed it and spun harder.

Tobias noticed the wheel clicked every time Lady McBeth's head was at the top of the wheel.

"Ready!" Lady McBeth shouted.

Magnus stood on a fifteen-foot long plywood runway. His left boot was out from his body. The toes of his boots were butted against raised strips of wood. He had six knives in his left hand and one knife in his throwing hand.

The spinning wheel clicked then clicked again...

Without hesitation Magnus flung the first knife. He snatched another knife and threw it with equal force. He kept flinging the knives.

Tobias could hear the metal striking the wood but the wheel was spinning so fast it was difficult to tell where the blades were landing. Hopefully not in Lady McBeth. At one point he almost looked away, fearing for her safety.

Magnus threw his last knife. "You may stop the wheel," he said, presumably to Tobias.

Tobias waited for the exact moment and grabbed the footplate, stopping the wheel. Lady McBeth smiled at him. The seven knives outlined her torso and legs, the blades missing her by no less than six inches.

"Oh my God, that was incredible," Tobias said.

"Sure you won't give it a try?" Lady McBeth asked.

Tobias was tempted if only to impress the beautiful assistant but the Spinning Wheel of Death was too dangerous.

"How about the balloon pop?" Half-Pint said.

"What's that?" Tobias asked.

"You hold a balloon and Magnus pops it with a knife."

"Gee, I don't know..."

"Come on, it'll be fun," Half-Pint persisted.

"Okay."

"This way," Lady McBeth said. She guided Tobias by the arm over to another plywood runway where an eight-foot by four-foot sheet of plywood was propped upright at the end. Red five-point stars were painted in a rectangle pattern six inches from the edges.

Magnus positioned himself on the runway and pulled a knife from his belt.

Lady McBeth blew up a balloon. She tied off the end and handed the blown-up balloon to Tobias.

"So what now?"

"I want you to stand right here at the edge of the backboard."

Tobias butted his right boot against the plywood.

"Perfect. Here, now put the balloon between your lips."

Tobias gawked at Lady McBeth. "I thought I was going to hold it with my hand."

"There's nothing to worry about," assured Lady McBeth.

Tobias glanced over at the mural on the side of the motor home of Magnus the Magnificent. "He's not going to wear that hood is he?"

"No."

"All right." Tobias put the knotted part of the balloon in his mouth. Lady McBeth moved him closer to the backboard until he was on the right spot.

"He's ready, Magnus," Lady McBeth called out.

Magnus raised his throwing hand.

Tobias could feel Lady McBeth's reassuring hand on his shoulder. "Magnus only wears the hood during a performance to thrill the audience."

"But he can still see through it, right?" Tobias managed to say between clinched teeth knowing it had to be rigged.

Lady McBeth let out a laugh. "Didn't you know? Magnus is blind."

Magnus pitched his arm forward and released the knife.

14

ROLO AND SAMSON

"That wasn't funny," Tobias said, so mad he wanted to punch the dwarf in the nose.

"You should have seen the expression on your face when that balloon popped," Half-Pint said. He and Penny couldn't stop laughing. They sounded like a couple of chattering squirrels.

"Why didn't you tell me Magnus was blind?"

"And ruin the act. No way."

"No more tricks, okay."

"Sure thing Mr. Morgan. Hey, no hard feelings." Half-Pint held out his chubby hand.

Tobias contemplated for a moment then decided to let bygones be bygones. He shook Half-Pint's chubby hand. "Ow, what the..."

The little bastard's wearing a hand buzzer.

"What'd you do that for?"

"It's what we clowns do."

"Should have known." Tobias rubbed his palm. He looked around and saw the roustabouts making good progress setting up the circus. They had a tent on a corner of his irrigation pond so the bleachers were facing the water. "Why'd they put a tent there?"

"It's for the Kelpie," Penny said.

"You're not supposed to tell." Half-Pint punched her in the shoulder. "Quit it."

"What's a Kelpie?" asked Tobias.

"What a minute. Did you hear something?" Half-Pint said, cupping his hand by his ear.

"I didn't hear..." then Tobias heard a double knock and a tinny voice.

"Excuse me, excuse me. Will you let me out of here?"

Tobias looked around but didn't see anyone nearby. "Where's that coming from?"

"Excuse me, excuse me. Will you let me out of here?"

"There's someone in that box," Penny said, pointing to what looked like a mechanic's tool chest on casters. Two more knocks sounded from inside.

"Excuse me, excuse me. Will you let me out of here?"

"That's impossible, there's no way anyone could fit in there," Tobias said. "This is another one of your pranks. There's a tape player inside."

"See for yourself," Half-Pint challenged Tobias.

Tobias reached down, flipped the two clasps, and opened the lid.

A face scowled up at him. "Well, it's about time!"

"Holy shit!" Tobias stumbled back and fell butt-first on the ground.

Half-Pint and Penny couldn't stop giggling. Finally, Half-Pint got his composure and said, "Say hello to Rollo the Rubberman."

Tobias got to his feet and looked down into the tool chest. "How did you even get in there?" Tobias asked Rollo. The man's arms were behind his head and his legs looked like stacked firewood.

"Easy. By dislocating my shoulders and hips."

"That has to hurt."

"It does. My back's killing me. You guys mind helping me out?"

"Sure thing, Rollo." Half-Pint and Tobias carefully lifted the human pretzel out of the tool chest. Rollo snapped his joints back into place. He stood tall and stretched his arms, popping every vertebra in his back. "Thank you very much. I think I'll go to my trailer, pop some Motrin, and lie down for a while."

Tobias watched Rollo walk stiffly to his trailer. "Is he going to be okay?"

"Sure," Half-Pint said. "He just has to get out the kinks."

"So when do I get to see the animals?"

"Ah, I don't think the boss would like that."

"Come on," Tobias begged. "Just one."

Half-Pint looked at Penny. She gave him a shrug.

"Okay, just one. And you better not rat on us."

"So where is it?"

"Over by that truck." Half-Pint grabbed Penny's hand and they led the way.

Tobias noticed it was one of the trucks with the canvas covers. The tarp on the back had been raised up revealing a large cage with straw on the floor. There didn't appear to be an animal inside. "I don't see anything."

Tobias heard a gruff snort behind him.

A sound a gorilla might make.

He slowly turned and stared up at the enormous creature before him.

"This is our strongman," Half-Pint said proudly.

"But it's a..."
"That's right. Meet Samson the Bigfoot."

15

STREET SWEEPERS

Mack and Anna wanted to be thorough with their investigation and decided not to leave any rock unturned so they had Sheriff Gooding take them to the spot where Suzie's car had been found. After walking the perimeter to get a sense of what Suzie and her friend Cindy experienced that night, the agents asked the sheriff to drive them to the small compound behind the Texaco station where Suzie's car had been towed.

The agents donned plastic gloves but didn't spend too much time searching through the vehicle, as it wasn't directly linked to Suzie's disappearance.

Afterward, the sheriff took them to the street where Cindy had last seen Suzie before she disappeared.

"So which house is the Fryer's?" Anna asked, climbing out the rear door of the police cruiser while Mack got out the front passenger side.

"That would be the beige house down the end of the street," Sheriff Gooding said, stepping in front of his vehicle and pointing.

Anna turned around slowly and studied the neighborhood of older homes sprawled on barren lots.

Mack stared down the opposite direction. "That's the corner where Cindy saw Suzie last?"

"That's right," Sheriff Gooding replied.

"And no one saw or heard anything that night?"

"I interviewed everyone on this street. Nothing."

"And there was no evidence of a struggle inside the house?" Mack asked.

"No, I believe I stated that in my report."

"So, if Suzie was abducted, it most likely happened here in the street," Anna said.

Mack nodded in agreement. "We better cover the area with a fine-toothed comb."

The sheriff opened the trunk of his cruiser. He handed out plastic gloves and large evidence bags. He shut the trunk.

Sheriff Gooding crossed over to the opposite side of the street while Mack went one way and Anna the other on their side.

For the next fifteen minutes, the sheriff and agents canvassed the sidewalks and gutters searching for clues. They returned to the cruiser to share their findings.

Candy wrappers and crushed beer cans mostly.

"I found some cigarette butts and an empty pack," Sheriff Gooding said.

"May I see that?" Anna took the evidence bag from the sheriff and studied the contents. "We have evidence Elroy left behind on the case we told you about." She stared at the empty soft pack of Lucky Strikes and cigarette butts. "We'll need to get this to our lab ASAP."

16

CHECK IN

Anna and Mack arrived at their motel just before nightfall. They'd stayed in worst places, this one most likely earning a social media three-star rating. The doors to the rooms faced out onto the tarmac parking lot of the L-shaped two-story building. A fenced-in swimming pool surrounded with some chaise lounge chairs was at one end.

Mack walked into the office while Anna sat in the rental car outside.

"How can I help you?" asked the young man at the desk.

"I believe I have a reservation," Mack said. He was beat from the late morning flight, the long drive to Buckhorn, and assisting the sheriff with the investigation.

When Anna had suggested sending the evidence they had found to the FBI Crime Lab, Mack had no idea how they would get it there from the remote border town.

Luckily, the sheriff knew of a private pilot who had a plane at a small airport not too far away. He made a quick call and Shelly rushed the evidence bag over. Anna got on her cell phone and made arrangements for an FBI agent to meet the pilot once he landed at Double Eagle II Airport, an aviation facility on the west side of Albuquerque International Sunport Airport.

As it was an active kidnapping, Anna got the lab to put a rush on analyzing the DNA on the cigarette butts found in the street to see if it matched with John Paul Elroy.

"It should be listed under Hunter," Mack said. "Or maybe Rivers. I'm not sure."

Mack caught the young man behind the desk looking suspiciously outside at Anna in the car.

"Is that your girlfriend?" the young man asked, glancing at the computer screen and typing on the keyboard.

"She's a colleague of mine."

"Company policy requires she register if she is staying in the motel."

"What?" Mack had to laugh. Don't tell me this guy thinks she's a hooker. "Come on, pal." Mack was bone-tired. He could feel his irritation meter rising. "Just give us the rooms."

"Rooms?" The young man took another look at the computer screen. "Oh, you booked two separate rooms."

"That's right. No funny business," Mack said wondering why he was letting this kid get under his skin. He couldn't have been more than nineteen years old. Probably his very first job.

"If she's having her own room, I'll definitely have to see her driver's license."

"For god's sake."

"They're the rules. Please, you have to understand I'm only doing my job," the young man said with a pained look on his face.

"Fine." Mack turned and signaled for Anna to come inside. She frowned and shook her head but when he waved at her again, she reluctantly got out of the car. He knew she was tired and not in a great mood and just wanted to take a shower and relax with the bottle of Jameson he knew she had packed in her tote bag.

"Is there a problem?" Anna asked, storming into the office.

"He needs to see your identification," Mack said, stepping back to view the fireworks.

Anna unclipped her FBI badge from her belt and shoved the shield in the young man's face. "Will this do?"

The clerk's eyes turned into saucers. "Uh, yeah, sorry I didn't mean to—"

Anna put out her hand. "Keycards!"

Fumbling behind the desk, the young man finally came up with the two plastic access cards and handed them to Anna. "Rooms 210 and 211. Enjoy your stay."

* * *

Mack knew Anna was tired and offered to take her travel bag up to her room but she declined the offer and carried it up herself. As soon as he entered his own room, Mack dropped his suitcase on the floor and flopped on the bed.

He must have dozed off because when he opened his eyes and checked the time on his cell phone, he had been asleep for more than an hour.

He got up, grabbed his suitcase off the floor and tossed it onto the bed. He unzipped the bag, took out some fresh clothes, and laid them on the bedspread.

Mack kicked off his shoes, unbuttoning his shirt as he walked into the small bathroom with the intent of turning on the shower.

"You've got to be kidding me," he said when he saw there were no fresh bath towels on the rack, only a tiny face towel on the counter next to a short stack of plastic cups wrapped in cellophane and two miniature bottles of shampoo and body wash.

Mack came back out to the room. He considered using the hotel phone and calling down to the office to have someone run up some towels when he noticed another door next to the dresser bureau with the flat screen TV. He had no idea his room had an adjoining door to the room Anna was occupying. Maybe she had an extra towel he could use.

He went over and unlocked the door. He opened the door and found another door. He figured it was locked but reached down anyway and was surprised to find it unlocked when he turned the knob. He pushed the door open slightly.

Anna paraded out of the bathroom with a towel wrapped around her; hair dripping wet from a shower. Mack couldn't take his eyes off her bare tan legs, muscular from her frequent jogs. He watched Anna step across the carpet to the small round table by the window.

She picked up a plastic cup and took a big gulp.

Mack knocked on the door and pushed it open wider. "You're not going to believe this, but there're no towels in my room. I was wondering if I could get one of yours."

"How long have you been peeking through the door?"

"Not long."

Anna placed the cup on the table. She took a deep breath and marched over to the door. "Will this one do?" She stripped off her towel and flung it in Mack's face.

Mack saw only white and stepped back as the door slammed.

"Go take a cold shower," Anna said laughingly from the other side of the door. "Then come meet me down at the pool."

17

THE COOKHOUSE

"Nightsinger says you're the guest of honor," Half-Pint said, holding hands with Penny as Tobias followed them over to the mess tent lit up with different colored strings of outdoor tiki lights. Two cooks grilled hamburgers and steaks while servers dished food out to the circus crew waiting in line as if it was a company picnic.

Everyone took their trays to the 40-foot long table with benches, covered with checkered table cloths and set up Basque-style so they could enjoy each other's company while eating. Bottles of red wine and glasses were provided on the table. The dining hall was abuzz with conversation and frequent laughter.

Half-Pint and Penny walked Tobias up to the first server. The word must have gotten out because no one complained or accused them of cutting in line. They each grabbed a tray and a plate and held it out as their turn came up. Tobias' mouth watered at the juicy 8-ounce steak put on his plate, then the generous helping of steaming fried rice mixed with scrambled egg, and a big square of buttered cornbread.

The dwarf couple escorted Tobias to the head of the table where J.J. Nightsinger was sitting. Tobias put his tray down and sat on the end of the bench next to the ringmaster. Half-Pint sat next to him while Penny sat on the bench across from Tobias.

"Evening, Tobias," Nightsinger said.

Half-Pint grabbed the nearest bottle and poured wine into three glasses. He handed Tobias his and gave Penny her wine.

Nightsinger pushed back his chair and stood. He raised his glass.

Everyone stopped talking and turned their attention to the lanky man in the top hat and red coat at the end of the table. They grabbed their own glasses and hoisted them in the air.

"Because Mr. Morgan has been so gracious, I have decided to make him an honorary cirky. What do you say?"

"Hear, hear!" belted an agreeing chorus.

Nightsinger smiled and drank from his wine.

Everyone at the table followed suit and tipped their glasses. After they lowered their glasses each person gave Tobias a warm smile like he was family.

Tobias hoped the silly grin on his face didn't make him look too goofy. He'd never been the center of attention before. Let alone accepted by such an altruistic group of people.

Nightsinger remained standing and looked down at Tobias. "Enjoy your meal. I'm sorry I can't stay but I have a circus to run."

"I understand, and thanks," Tobias said, his heart swelling, like an unknown suddenly thrust into celebrity status.

18

52-CARD PICKUP

After a hearty meal, Half-Pint and Penny took Tobias over to their motor home facing out at the other trailers and RVs positioned in half circles around fire pits so everyone could relax and enjoy the evening. While Tobias made himself comfortable on a folding lawn chair, Half-Pint and Penny ducked inside their trailer. Half-Pint came out carrying two bottled beers. He popped the caps off and handed one to Tobias then sat in the chair next to the farmer.

Tobias heard the drone of the gas generators providing power to the surrounding lights. He saw different groups gathered at the fire pits or sitting around tables. He was curious who they were so he asked Half-Pint if he would point people out.

Half-Pint gulped down some beer. He motioned to a blonde woman sitting on the steps of a motor home. She wore a lavender outfit with long white sleeves and a series of yellow brads down the front of her chest. Her thigh-high boots were a shade lighter than her costume.

Tobias glanced in the general direction. "Who is she?"

"That's Andrea."

"What does she do?"

"She handles the big cats."

"What, like a lion tamer?"

"No, not lions. You'll see come show time."

"What about those guys?" Tobias asked recognizing the burly sledge gang that was driving the stakes into the ground around the tents. They sat at a small table playing cards and passing around a bottle.

"See the big Polynesian with all the tribal tattoos?"

"Yeah."

"That's Keko Mander. The big black guy next to him is Bubba Root. He was a heavyweight boxer until he put some poor sucker in a coma. The other guy is Lou Stone, used to be an Olympic bodybuilder."

"Who's the smaller one sitting next to him?"

"That's Armand Carson. He's Samson's handler," Half-Pint said.

"You mean the Bigfoot has a trainer?"

"Oh, he's much more than that."

Tobias looked at the fifth man at the table. "And the one with the stogie?"

"That's the roustabouts' foreman, Rocky Hardman. Tough as nails. Used to be a longshoreman before he joined up."

Tobias gazed around at the other camps. He spotted Magnus and Lady McBeth sitting by their own fire pit. He saw Rollo's camper with a light on inside. "You know, when you guys first drove up, there was a woman in the front seat with Nightsinger. I don't see her."

"That would be Belen. She keeps to herself mostly, especially at night," Half-Pint said, draining his beer. He turned and pounded on the aluminum siding by the door. "Can we get another beer?" He looked at Tobias. "You ready?"

"Sure," Tobias said, and finished his beer.

Half-Pint yelled out, "Make that two."

Seconds later the door flung open and tiny feet came down the steps. "Two beers coming up," said a voice Tobias didn't recognize. It was another dwarf Tobias hadn't yet met.

"This here's Slappy," Half-Pint said. Slappy wore the same identical outfit as Half-Pint but was slightly bigger. His face makeup was like Half-Pint's but he wore a red wig instead of a yellow one and had a receding hairline.

Slappy flipped the two beers in the air and caught them.

"Real funny," Half-Pint said, snatching a bottle. He held it out and popped the cap. White foam gushed out the spout. He put the end of the bottle up to his mouth but it went all over his face.

Tobias slowly unscrewed his cap and the suds spurted out onto the front of his shirt.

Another dwarf came out. He laughed when he saw Tobias and Half-Pint drenched in beer.

"And this clown is Pogo," Half-Pint said, wiping his face. "He's our gnome wrangler." Pogo was the spitting image of Slappy only a couple of inches shorter.

"Gnome? What, like garden statues?" Tobias asked dubiously.

"No."

"Then what are they?"

"Little critters we discovered in Spain..."

Half-Pint put his chubby hand over Pogo's mouth. "Keep your trap shut."

"Come on, Slappy, I know when a guy's not wanted." Pogo headed back inside the motor home. Slappy went in after him.

"Dad!" a young dwarf called out and came down to the bottom step. He was young, maybe fourteen; Tobias couldn't really say for sure. He wore clown makeup with a big grin drawn on his face and a tight-mesh green wig. His costume was similar to the others with sewn quilt work on his shirt and the knees of his pants.

"This is my son, Patches," Half-Pint said.

"Nice to meet you," Tobias said.

Patches gave Tobias a little wave. If he smiled, Tobias couldn't tell as his mouth was locked into a permanent grin.

"Mom says don't stay up too late."

"You tell her I'll be in shortly."

Patches turned and went back inside the motor home.

"I've got a question," Tobias said to Half-Pint.

"What's that?"

"Don't you guys ever take off your makeup?"

"Who says it's makeup?" Half-Pint pointed to another group of clowns clustered around a fire pit.

From what Tobias could tell, they were regular sized adults still in their costumes even though the main performance wasn't until tomorrow evening. He wondered if they had worn them for a rehearsal. Surely they would take them off before going to bed.

Tobias heard shouting from the card game. Bubba Root jumped up from the table while the other men remained in their chairs.

"I saw you pull that card out of your sleeve," Bubba accused Armand.

"You're seeing things," Armand snapped back.

"Bubba sit down," Rocky said, chomping on his cigar as he stared up at the angry man.

"Not until he admits he cheated!"

"Maybe you need your eyes checked," Armand said.

"Maybe you need me to use your head for a punching bag."

"Uh-oh," Half-Pint said, watching the ruckus.

"Bubba, sit the hell down!" Rocky yelled.

"Yeah man," Keko said. "Better do what the man says before there's big trouble."

Bubba scowled at Armand and punched the palm of his hand. "How would you like it if this was your face?"

Armand grinned up at Bubba. "You shouldn't have said that."

The encampment suddenly went quiet.

Tobias heard heavy footsteps approaching. A huge figure charged out of the dark and crashed into the card table knocking it onto its side, scattering playing cards and chips. The men in their chairs jumped up and scattered as the eight-foot tall Bigfoot grabbed Bubba by the throat and lifted the big man off the ground.

"Still want to call me a cheater?" Armand said.

Bubba couldn't breathe, let alone reply. He made a futile attempt to pry the creature's fingers from his neck but they were coiled steel around his throat. His eyes rolled back as he kicked his feet.

"Armand, order him to release Bubba," Rocky shouted. "Now!"

"Come on, Armand." Keko took a step to help his friend but stopped when he saw the Bigfoot bare his teeth.

Samson raised Bubba even higher. The ex-boxer's eyes fluttered and he passed out.

"All right, Samson, let him go," Armand instructed the big beast.

Samson opened his fingers and Bubba hit the ground with a heavy thud.

Keko rushed over to see if Bubba was still breathing.

"You almost killed him," Keko yelled at the giant Sasquatch once he found a pulse.

"You need to keep him under control," Rocky said.

"Tell that to your men." Armand tugged on the Bigfoot's arm. "Come on, Samson, time to turn in." He walked off with the Bigfoot lumbering beside him.

"What was that all about?" As surprised as Tobias was by the squabble, he knew there was always unrest in the best of families.

"Sometimes these guys forget," Half-Pint said.

"Forget what?"

"That it's not smart to mess with a handler. You see circus handlers have a special bond with their performers."

"You mean their animals."

"I wouldn't exactly call them that," Half-Pint said.

19

POSTING THE BILLS

Even though the sun had been down for almost two hours, it was still warm enough for Mack to wear a T-shirt and cargo shorts. The bath towel he had used after his shower had been damp from Anna but he didn't mind, as he could still smell her scent on his skin.

He clipped his holster on the waistband of his shorts and concealed the Glock under his T-shirt. Regulations required that he kept his firearm with him at all times along with his badge especially as there wasn't a security safe in his room. He slipped on a pair of canvas deck shoes and left the room.

He walked along the balcony by the other rooms and went down the concrete steps. He followed the walkway to the fenced-in pool. He opened the gate and spotted Anna by the deep end, sitting on a chaise lounge in a lightweight sundress with her legs stretched out, a plastic cup on her lap. Her tote bag was on the cement next to her within reach. Mack figured she had the bottle of Jameson in the bag along with her service pistol.

"Any word from the lab?" Mack said, occupying the reclining chair next to his partner.

Anna patted her cell phone resting on her right thigh. "No, nothing yet."

She poured him three fingers of Jameson and handed Mack the plastic cup. He took a sip of whiskey. It burned his throat but he knew after a few more swallows it would have a numbing effect and wouldn't be as harsh.

Mack gazed around the pool area and didn't see anyone else. "I guess we have the place to ourselves."

"Pool hours were over an hour ago."

"Hope our friend from the front desk doesn't do rounds."

"I can't believe I'm doing this," Anna said, leaning back and staring up at the stars.

"Doing what?"

"This." She took a drink of her whiskey. "I almost feel guilty."

"Key word 'almost.'"

"Yeah. Do those things ever shut up?"

Mack turned to a nearby tree on the other side of the fence where thousands of buzzing cicadas were stuck in a continuous replay of the same pattern of sounds like someone repeatedly scratching their fingernail over a sheet of paper. "Did you know cicadas spend up to thirteen years living underground before they become adults?"

"Shame they don't stay there." Anna took another drink.

"In a way you have to feel sorry for them."

"And why's that?"

"What if you had only four to six weeks to mate and then you died?"

"Then I would say I died happy." Anna gulped down the rest of her whiskey. She reached inside her tote bag, took out the bottle of Jameson, and poured herself another drink.

"How many of those have you had?" Mack asked.

"Why, are you—" Anna paused when her cell phone chimed. She picked it up and pressed the phone against her ear. "Hello? Yes, this is Special Agent Rivers." Anna listened for a few seconds. "Great. Thank you so much. Bye."

"Was that them?"

Anna grinned. "It was a match. Looks like our man was in town."

"We better let the sheriff know." Mack reached in his pocket and took out his phone.

* * *

Joseph had made his first sweep of the town when his cell phone rang on the dock next to his cup holder. He grabbed his phone and pulled over to the side of the road.

"This is Sheriff Gooding." It was Special Agent Hunter. Joseph listened while Hunter told him the FBI Lab had confirmed the DNA on the cigarette butts found in the street near Suzie Fryer's house was indeed that of the same person that the agents were after. He thanked Hunter for letting him know and ended the call. It was time to put out a statewide manhunt for John Paul Elroy.

Joseph was about to pull out onto the road when a figure on a unicycle raced by and threw something through the open window of the cruiser and hit Joseph in the face.

"Hey!" Joseph yelled. He looked down and saw a rolled-up tube of paper on the passenger seat. He glanced in his side mirror. The unicyclist was pedaling like his legs were quick-firing pistons and made a quick turn at the corner.

"No, you don't." Joseph cranked the steering wheel and stomped on the accelerator. The cruiser spun in a half circle, burning a small patch of rubber. Joseph straightened the wheel and tromped on the gas pedal. If he had been in a high-speed chase he would have sounded the siren and switched on the roof lights. He couldn't justify chasing a man on a unicycle with a 250 horsepower car being much of a high-speed pursuit.

He turned down the street of homes with rock garden frontages and slowed down, having lost sight of the unicyclist.

Where did he go?

Joseph turned on his spotlight mounted on the front of the driver door. Gripping the handle, he made a sweep of the left-hand side of the street. Nothing. He shined the beam up the opposite walkway and saw no sign of the unicyclist. He wished he had gotten a better look at the rider, as he had no idea what he looked like.

He kept the spotlight on and coasted up the street.

That's when he saw the posters. They were affixed to tree trunks and lampposts.

As he went down the street and turned onto another block, he saw more of them.

After driving twenty minutes it seemed like they were everywhere.

Joseph pulled over to the curb and put the cruiser in park. He grabbed the scroll of paper off the passenger seat. He reached up and turned on his dome light. He unrolled the paper, laid it flat on the steering wheel, and read the poster.

CRYPTID CIRCUS

THE MOST AMAZING SHOW IN THE WORLD
UNDER THE BIG TOP
UNIQUE ACTS AND INCREDIBLE CREATURES
THRILLS AND CHILLS FOR EVERYONE
CONSESSION STANDS AND GAME BOOTHS
AT THE MORGAN FARM ON ROUTE 9
PLENTY OF PARKING
COME ONE, COME ALL

TICKETS SOLD AT THE TICKET BOOTH

---

* * *

Anna stood in front of the bathroom sink and splashed water on her face. She needed to be clear-headed for tomorrow. She hadn't intended on polishing off the bottle of Jameson—with Mack's help of course—but it felt good to unwind. She wondered if he felt as bad as she did. Nothing a good night's rest wouldn't fix. She glanced at the clock radio on the stand by the bed. It read 12:13. She figured she might be able to squeeze in maybe four or five hours sleep.

She was about to slip her sundress over her head when there was a knock at the door to her room. She reached into her tote bag and took out her handgun. She approached the door slowly and gazed out the peephole.

There was no one there.

She heard a bang outside on the next door down. She pulled her door open and slipped out onto the balcony.

She caught a glimpse of a figure and raised her gun.

"Whoa, it's me," Mack said.

They turned and saw a small creature running down the hand railing and disappear around the corner of the building.

"What the hell was that? A giant rat?" Mack picked up the poster left by his door.

"I don't know. What do you have there?" Anna said.

"You're not going to believe it. It's an announcement for a circus."

"Where?"

"Somewhere out on Route 9. Must be near town."

"This might be our lucky break," Anna said.

"Yeah, where there's a circus..."

"There's a clown."

20

THE GAFFER

Mack sipped his coffee while driving their rental car down the desert road. He held his cup and the steering wheel with his left hand, reached up with his right, and flipped the sun visor down to shield the morning sun glaring on the windshield.

"So, what did the sheriff tell you when you called him?"

"The farm is owned by Tobias Morgan," Anna replied from the front passenger seat. She took a gulp of coffee. "He has over thirty acres. Grows wheat mostly. Wife deceased. No kids."

Mack spotted a farmhouse up ahead. "Is that it?"

"Looks like it."

As they drew closer, Mack could see the tops of the tents beyond the barn roof. A large fleet of semi trucks and numerous RV's were parked in various formations near the wheat field. He spotted Sheriff Gooding's patrol car on the side of the road by the front entrance to the driveway. The sheriff was by the farmhouse. He had a notepad out and was interviewing a shirtless Hawaiian man with intricate tattoos inked on his upper torso and both arms.

Mack turned down the driveway and parked next to the split rail fence. He placed his coffee cup in the console holder next to Anna's. They got out of the car and walked over to the two men.

Sheriff Gooding turned to the approaching agents. "Morning."

Mack and Anna greeted the sheriff.

"This is Keko Mander," the sheriff said. "He works with the circus."

Mack tried not to stare at the man's bulging muscles thinking he would be the perfect stand-in actor for Dwayne 'The Rock' Johnson. "Mr. Mander. Where could we find your boss?"

"Mr. Meyers? He'd be in the gaffer's trailer."

"The what?" Mack asked.

"He's the circus manager," the sheriff said, taking a peek at the notepad in his hand. "Hank Meyers. He owns and manages the operation."

"Can you take us to him?" Anna asked.

"I'm supposed to stay right here," Keko said. He unclipped a small portable two-way radio from his belt. He pressed the Talk button. "There are some people want to see the gaffer."

"Be right there," crackled a reply over the small speaker.

They didn't have to wait long before a man resembling Indiana Jones came their way wearing a high-crowned wide-brimmed sable fedora, a light khaki shirt under a worn leather jacket, and brown pants. But the closer he got, Mack realized he didn't look anything like Harrison Ford as the man had a black eye patch over his right eye and sported a black goatee. His nose was misshaped—possibly as a boxer— from being broken too many times and reset hastily.

"I'm Hank Meyers. If you're here about permits, I assure you they are all current."

"Well, I might have to—" the sheriff started before Mack cut him off.

"We're more interested in your employees."

"Oh?"

"His name is John Paul Elroy," Anna said.

"I'm sorry but I don't have anyone by that name employed here," Meyers replied.

"He works as a clown. Calls himself Koko."

"No. I have a troupe of clowns but none of my zanies go by Koko."

"Do you keep pictures of your employees?" Anna asked.

"Only in costume."

"May we see them?"

"If you like. Follow me."

Mack had never been to a circus, even as a child. Meyers took them through a gauntlet of activity, workers setting up booths and concession stands, performers parading about the back lots behind the main tent in different outfits and costumes.

Something seemed to be missing. "Where are the animals?" he asked.

"In their containments, feeding," Meyer said over his shoulder. He stopped at a trailer. "Please come in." He went up the three short steps and opened the door.

The front room was an office with a desk and filing cabinets. A couch and coffee table were positioned on one wall under a window. Mack and Anna sat on the couch. The sheriff chose to stand and wait while Meyers opened a file cabinet and rifled through the folders. He took out a folder and brought it over, placing it on the coffee table.

"I have nineteen clowns. Seven are dwarfs."

"Well, we can cross those seven off the list," Anna said. "Elroy's certainly not a dwarf."

Mack opened the file of 8-by-10 professional headshots used for auditioning.

They took their time and looked at each one. None looked anything like the psycho clown Koko from the warehouse.

"Damn," Mack said. "That was a bust."

21

GUARD SHACK

Camden Fryer looked up from the *Field and Stream* on his lap and gave the car cruising by the booth his customary wave. That made the twelfth car in the last hour. Not what he would call a mass exodus but it was more than what he normally witnessed on a Saturday morning. Usually the residents of Desert Sands Estates slept in, as most of them spent their workweeks commuting ungodly distances to work. Weekends were generally reserved for catching up on much needed sleep or tackling neglected chores.

He closed the magazine and shoved it into the shelf under the narrow desktop where he kept handbills for upcoming events or new regulation notices he was expected to hand out to the homeowners when entering the gated community.

Camden hadn't had much of an appetite since Suzie's disappearance.

He had joined the search party organized by the sheriff knowing there was no way he could sit home waiting for the inevitable phone call. They had covered a five-mile radius around Suzie's car, both on foot and in four-wheel drive vehicles. As much as he wanted desperately to find his daughter, a part of him dreaded what they might discover out in the desert.

Since the search was called off, he had no choice but to sit and wait while the police conducted the investigation. Sheriff Gooding had promised to keep him apprised of the case's progress but so far he hadn't heard a thing.

Camden even entertained the thought that Suzie's abduction might have resulted in a ransom demand though no one had tried to contact him. The kidnappers would have had better luck trying to squeeze blood out of a rock as he had little savings and was a month behind in the mortgage.

He felt like he was bouncing off the walls in the cramped guard shack. He needed to get some air. He grabbed the Cushman key off the hook, stepped out of the booth, and locked the sliding door. He climbed onto the seat of the electric golf cart parked in front of the cement island.

Inserting the key, he pressed his foot down on the pedal. He turned into the entrance lane, accelerating onto the street of recently constructed homes. Five-foot tall black steel rail fences ran up the sides of the houses and the rear property lines of the backyards, giving an airy appeal but offered no privacy. Camden could see sunbeams glistening off the surfaces of the swimming pools.

He turned right and stopped at the street sign. He saw another one of those posters. He was tempted to tear it down but figured what was the use. They were everywhere, on the streetlamps, at the recreation center, under windshield wipers, in every curbside mailbox.

It drove Camden crazy knowing the culprits had put them there while he was on watch and he had never seen a soul.

He knew he was going to catch some flack. It showed a lack of security if anyone could sneak into the protected community and hang posters wherever they pleased. What if they had been vandals tagging the community with spray-painted graffiti? That would have meant his job for sure.

Changing his mind, he tore the poster off the street signpost and crumbled it up in a ball.

He made his rounds around the gated neighborhood.

Every so often he would see folks standing in their front yards and driveways, talking excitedly about the circus that had just come to town.

22

BEANS AND MOLASSES

Suzie wasn't sure if she had drifted off to sleep or passed out from lack of air in the stuffy van. Her skin was slick with sweat. She was thankful he had removed her sweatshirt when he had first abducted her or she would have baked to death. Her tight-fitting jeans clung to her like a second skin. She wrinkled her nose, repulsed by her own body odor.

The van's interior reeked from the smell of paint, which she had earlier mistaken for gasoline. The moment she thought she was going to die.

She jerked, startled by the sudden opening of the rear doors.

Even with the burlap hood over her head, she still had to squint from the bright light. She heard him crawl inside. As he moved toward her, she could hear his labored breathing like he had just returned from a run. She smelled stale cigarette smoke and realized the real reason.

He yanked the hood off her head. She clamped her eyes shut, afraid to look him straight in the face.

"Open your eyes," he said and popped the ball gag out of her mouth.

"Please..." Her mouth was so dry.

"I said: Open your eyes!"

His stern tone compelled her to gaze into his face.

He looked like a sad hobo with the corners of his painted white lips turned down and the heavy 5 o'clock shadow charcoal makeup applied to his lower cheeks and chin.

His eyelids were blackened with mascara heightening his forlorn look and he had a small red rubber nose. His hair—what little he had of it—was wispy shocks over his ears. He wore a tattered jacket and shirt with a checkered tie.

"Well, what do you think?" he asked.

Suzie was too afraid to answer.

"Jocko asked you a question."

Even though he had a pitiful persona, she could see there was something menacing in those black eyes. Her heart fluttered like a hummingbird trapped in her chest. She knew at any moment she was going to pee herself.

He must have noticed her squirming because he reached up with a finely honed hunting knife and sliced through the plastic tie holding her arm up against the metal wall.

Her hand fell to her side. She shook her arm to return the circulation. She lowered her head. "Please, don't hurt me."

"Quiet. If you scream, I won't be nice."

"I won't, I promise."

"That's a good girl."

He leaned over and cut through the plastic tie around her left hand by her waist so that both her hands were free. He slipped the blade between her ankles and severed the rope. "Take off your clothes."

"Please..."

"I won't ask again."

Suzie couldn't hold back the tears. She untied her sneakers and pulled them off.

She unsnapped her jeans.

She looked down and saw two buckets, one empty and rusted inside, and the other full of soapy water with a rag draped over the rim.

"You know what to do." He backed away and climbed out of the van.

She could see his dark silhouette standing in the backdrop of bright sunlight.

The sick bastard was going to watch.

Suzie slipped off her jeans and briefs. She couldn't wait any longer and relieved herself in the bucket. Once she was done, he reached inside the van and dragged out the sloshing pail.

She took off her shirt and began lathering her naked body with the cold soapy water, hoping he wasn't watching. She closed her eyes and pretended he wasn't there though she could hear his heavy breathing.

Once she was through, she dropped the dirty rag back into the bucket.

"Put this on." He tossed a crumpled garment at her feet.

She opened her eyes and saw an old monogrammed T-shirt with the faded words **Carnival Extravaganza** on the front. Suzie picked up the shirt, poked her head through the neck opening, and pulled the top down to her thighs.

"Time to eat." He handed her an open can with a spoon sticking out.

She took it from him. The paper label had been removed. For all she knew, he was feeding her dog food but it didn't matter, as she was too hungry to care. She scooped a spoonful into her mouth. She was relieved to find it was juicy baked beans in molasses and was soothing sliding down her throat.

He put a plastic bottled water by her feet.

She put the can down and grabbed the bottle. She twisted off the cap and gulped half of it down until she choked. She coughed and gagged and drank some more. She put the bottle down between her feet and picked up the can.

She dove into the rest of the beans like it was the best thing she had ever eaten in her life. For all she knew, it might be the last thing she would ever have.

Suzie missed her dad so much. She wished by some miracle he would find her and hold her in his arms.

Right after he killed this damn clown.

She swooned and dropped the can and then the spoon. The bottle between her feet tipped over. Suzie stared at the water gurgling out the spout.

Not again.

She looked up and saw the blurry hobo smiling before she keeled over.

23

STEP RIGHT UP

Cindy Jacobs didn't know what was worse: having to come straight home from school every day for an entire month and being grounded to her room after being suspended for smoking in the girl's bathroom or spending an awkward outing with her parents. Ever since her suspension, her parents had been at odds to the best method of punishment. Her dad was notorious for being a lenient disciplinarian, her mother the strict enforcer.

She'd heard them arguing in the kitchen before they had gotten in the car.

"Don't you think she's been through enough," her father protested. "Her best friend is missing."

"Pete, quit trying to undermine my every decision. She got kicked out of school."

"It was only three days."

"The suspension will be on her record. What if it hurts her chances of getting into New Mexico State?"

"Then we'll worry about that when the time comes. Pam, can we just talk about this later? What do you say? Truce?"

"All right. But I'm leaving it for further discussion."

"Fair enough. Call Cindy down. We should get going."

"I have to admit, Pete, I am a little excited."

"You and me both. Let's go and have some fun. For Cindy's sake."

It was mid-afternoon when they reached the Morgan farm on Route 9 and saw a long string of cars waiting to enter the property. Her dad rolled up to the last car in line. "Looks like quite the turnout."

Cindy pressed the button on her armrest and lowered her window. She stuck her head out. She saw a man dressed up as a clown standing at the entry gate. He was taking money and waving cars through.

Her dad looked out his window when it was eventually their turn.

"Here're some free coupons for the midway," the clown said, and handed out the vouchers. "That'll be twenty dollars."

"What a minute, you just said they were free."

"They are. It's twenty bucks to park."

"That's a little steep."

The driver behind them gave his horn a curt tap.

"Sorry, buddy, you're holding up the line."

Cindy's dad grumbled and paid the clown.

Men with batons directed the arriving traffic into separate parking areas with two vehicles butted bumper to bumper in long rows, leaving enough space so they could either pull forward or back out into a lane when leaving the event.

Cindy's dad was directed to park with the other cars by the wheat field.

They got out of the car and walked along behind the other people heading over to the ticket booth in front of the main entrance. Cindy saw more than two hundred cars in the dirt lot.

Cindy stood behind her parents and gazed up at the ticket prices over the window. Adults were $40, children twelve and under $20. A family package was $75.

"The family package, please," Cindy's dad told the person in the ticket booth.

The circus calliope music played on the loud speakers as they entered the grounds. Kids of all ages were gathered in front of the fun booths throwing darts at balloons and tossing softballs into hoops to win prizes. Some were firing pellet guns at cardboard animals moving on a track at a shooting gallery.

The food concessions were packed with people buying hotdogs and hamburgers.

Watching everyone having fun was becoming contagious.

"Well?"

Cindy turned to her dad. "Well, what?"

"Ready for some fun?"

"Dad, I'm not a little kid."

"Ah, but the circus brings out the 'little kid' in all of us."

"Pete, quit harassing our daughter," Cindy's mom said.

"Since when is asking our daughter if she's ready to have some fun, harassing?"

"You know what I mean."

Cindy looked at her mother and saw her smiling.

They walked through the crowd toward the main tent: the big top. A billboard was set up at the entrance with the acts and the times of each show.

"Looks like we're in luck," Cindy's dad said, checking his wristwatch. "The next show is in ten minutes."

"Let's get a good seat." Cindy's mom hooked her arm inside Cindy's so they could walk in together.

Cindy felt giddy. Maybe this wasn't going to be such a bad day after all.

24

ANDREA'S CATS

Blue colored seats surrounded the main arena and tiered up ten rows high into the grandstand, enough to seat five hundred people. The interior was gloomy under the canvas with the exception of the spotlight shining on the center ring and sunlight coming in through the entrance between the turned back tent flaps.

Cindy and her parents sat together in the fifth row. Once they were in their chairs, Cindy glanced around and saw two-thirds of the seats were occupied and was not nearly a full house. She figured more people would show up later when it was dark and the circus was all lit up.

She saw kids munching on popcorn and eating strands of blue cotton candy.

The tent flaps closed suddenly, sealing off the entrance.

A dramatic score sounded on the loud speakers and the spotlight tracked a lone figure walking into the center ring. He wore a black top hat, short red jacket, brown pants, and black shin-high boots.

The music ended abruptly and the audience went quiet.

"Ladies and Gentlemen, and children of all ages! I am J.J. Nightsinger—Your Ringmaster," Nightsinger shouted into the microphone. "Welcome to Cryptid Circus!"

The ringmaster's jubilance gathered much applause and whistling.

"What you are about to see goes beyond the realm of the imagination. I give you the fearless Andrea and her amazing Maltese tigers: Somba and Rumba!" He stepped away and disappeared into the shadows.

Cindy sat forward in her seat with anticipation.

The spotlight lit up the archway facing the arena.

A giant tiger emerged. It was blue with dark gray stripes. Even though she had never seen such an animal before—not even in a zoo— Cindy thought the beast seemed abnormally huge. It was much larger than a Holstein bull and had to weigh more than half a ton.

A second big cat crept into the arena, even bigger than the first feline.

Andrea paraded into the ring, wearing a tight-fitting lavender costume with yellow brads on the chest and riding boots.

She held a long riding crop in each hand. She cracked the whips and yelled, "Somba! Rumba! Up!"

The bigger cat, Somba, jumped onto a steel platform facing the audience. Rumba leaped onto a metal stand ten feet away positioned in front of the crowd.

Cindy heard her mother say, "My God, they're letting them roam free with no cage."

"You're right," her father said. "What's to stop them from jumping into the seats?"

More people began to utter concerns.

Andrea stepped between the humongous tigers. She looked up at the nervous crowd, smiled, and shouted, "Somba! Rumba! Speak!"

Both tigers rose up on their hind legs at the exact same moment with their front paws in the air. Each one stood over fifteen feet tall.

Somba and Rumba sucked in deep breaths and exhaled fierce roars.

Cindy and the rest of the audience drew back in their seats.

"Down!" Andrea shouted.

The colossal tigers sat back down on the platforms.

"I assure you Somba and Rumba are quite safe. And to prove it, perhaps I could get a volunteer from the audience to demonstrate?"

Cindy didn't see any show of hands.

"No?" Andrea said disappointedly. "Then I must choose."

Afraid they might be picked, many people averted their eyes from the trainer.

"What about you, young lady? Would you like to come down?"

Cindy looked around, expecting someone to stand up. Everyone remained seated.

She turned her attention back to the center ring. Andrea was looking up into the stands, staring directly at Cindy.

"Me? No, I don't think so." Cindy turned to her mother. "Mom?"

"Honey, you don't have to go."

"What is your name?" Andrea shouted.

"Cindy," Cindy yelled back after some hesitation.

"Cindy. Come and say hello to Somba and Rumba."

Before Cindy could decline a young voice in the audience yelled, "Cindy, Cindy."

And then another person joined in and soon everyone was chanting "Cindy" over and over again.

Wanting them to stop, Cindy slowly rose from her seat.

"That's a girl!" a man shouted from the back.

Cindy saw her dad scowl and look over his shoulder like he was ready to rip the guy's head off.

"Honey, sit down." Her mother put her hand on Cindy's arm.

"It's okay Mom." Cindy scooted past the people in the next seats to the aisle. She went down the steps and entered the ring where Andrea stood between the two cats on the pedestals.

"Thank you for being so brave," Andrea said.

"Please don't ask me to put my head in their mouths."

Andrea laughed. "No, I would never do that. Stand by my side while I coax them down."

Cindy stood close to the trainer. Andrea snapped her whip and shouted, "Somba! Come!"

The giant tiger leaped from the platform in a mighty bound, straight over Andrea and Cindy's heads. Cindy gazed up at the powerful beast's underbelly as it soared over landing in the center of the ring and lay on its belly.

Andrea flicked her whip. "Rumba! Come!"

Rumba vaulted over them and came down, lying beside Somba.

Cindy was amazed by the way the big cats willingly responded to Andrea's commands like pets eager to please a master with a treat in hand. As Andrea didn't seem to be rewarding the tigers with food snacks, Cindy could only assume there was some kind of special bond of adoration between the trainer and her performers.

"Would you like to sit between them?" Andrea asked.

"Uh, I don't know."

"It's perfectly fine." Andrea took Cindy's hand and guided her over to Somba and Rumba. The big cats watched Cindy intently. They kept rock-still like a pair of statues outside the cement steps of a museum.

Cindy did as Andrea instructed and sat down between the massive beasts' shoulders. She had to gaze up to see the sides of their faces, lips curled to show off their saber tooth long fangs.

Somba shifted his body closer to Rumba, squeezing Cindy in the middle. At first she wanted to call out in alarm but then she realized the gargantuan tiger only wanted to cuddle next to her much like an affectionate housecat. She reached up with both hands and kneaded their blue fur with her fingers.

Both cats responded by heaving their chests and moaning like a pair of wallowing calves.

Andrea raised her arms in the air signaling the need for applause from the audience. Everyone cheered and clapped their hands.

Andrea thanked Cindy and sent her back to her seat.

Her parents were so ecstatic, her mom gave her a kiss on the cheek.

Cindy had never been so scared and excited at the same time. Being part of the act was an experience she would never forget.

She watched with a new reverent interest as Somba and Rumba continued their routines.

25

ARMAND AND SAMSON

Tobias had no idea the circus would be such a success. He'd never seen so many cars parked on his land, and they were still rolling in. With parking fees, admission, and the take from the game booths and concession stands, he could definitely expect to make enough money to fix his tractor from his share of the proceeds.

And they were only getting started. Nightsinger boasted the night take would be even bigger.

Walking around the bustling crowds, Tobias spotted some farmers he knew from the auctions at the grange, some that even lived in the next county, enjoying their time with their families.

He couldn't help wondering how so many people had found out about the opening on such short notice as the circus didn't have a website on the Internet. The only thing he could think of was the traveling circus must have left posters along their route advertising the actual location where they would perform. But then how did they know what information to put on the posters unless they had already mapped it out and secured the grounds?

Which meant Nightsinger had to have been cocksure Tobias would agree to his sales pitch long before arriving at his farm. It was a widely publicized fact that farmers in the region were struggling to make ends meet so it was no surprise Tobias didn't turn down the offer. Soon he would be raking in a nice bit of change from the purse.

He stopped by the concession stand selling hotdogs. The man working inside saw Tobias and waved him to the window next to the one serving a long line of people.

Tobias was rather enjoying the preferential treatment.

"So what would you like on your wiener, Mr. Morgan?"

A young couple burst out laughing at the head of the line at the next window.

Tobias gave the man inside the concession stand a blank look.

"On your frankfurter, your sausage. What do you want? Mustard, catsup, pickles?"

"Oh, mustard is fine."

"Here you go." The man handed Tobias a foot long with mustard squiggles. "On the house."

Tobias started to walk away when a voice said, "Nice event you're hosting." He turned and saw Sheriff Gooding standing with his wife, Shelly. They were both in uniform.

"Uh, hi sheriff. You two care for some food?" Tobias took a big bite of his hotdog.

"Not right now," Sheriff Gooding said. "I went down to the courthouse to pull your permits. And guess what?"

Tobias nearly choked. He didn't know anything about having to apply for any permits. The last thing he needed was for the sheriff to shut them down and impose a heavy fine. He'd be worse off than before.

He managed to swallow. "Ah, sheriff, no one ever—"

Sheriff Gooding raised his hand to stop Tobias from speaking and pulled an envelope from his back pocket to show Tobias. "I'm here to tell you everything's in order. Seems a Mr. J.J. Nightsinger provided all the necessary paperwork."

Tobias was flabbergasted. "Is that so."

"How late do you plan to keep the circus operating tonight?"

"I believe to midnight."

The sheriff glanced at his wristwatch. "Looks like you've got another six hours." He looked at Tobias. "Shelly and I are here to make sure there's no trouble."

"Well, thank you, sheriff."

"Don't mention it. Enjoy your evening."

Tobias turned and walked away. He finished his hotdog in two bites.

A large group of people had congregated by the irrigation ditch running parallel to the wheat field. Tobias saw Armand standing on a platform so he could be seen over the heads of the crowd.

"What man here wants to challenge Samson to a tug-a-war? If so, step right up to the rope on this side of the ditch."

Tobias heard some chatter in the crowd.

A man stepped out, rolling up his sleeves. Tobias recognized Kenny Thompson as he had hired the man once for a harvest. Thompson proved to be a drunk and would show up late for work. He was also a troublemaker and liked to pick fights with the other men, so Tobias had let him go.

Another man lumbered over to the rope that extended across the trench to the edge of the wheat field. Tobias didn't know his name but by the way the man joked with Thompson they were acquaintances.

"That's right, line up," Armand said. "Come on now," he yelled to the crowd. "We need eight more men, ten in total of your town's strongest men."

"What, one man against ten?" someone yelled. "That's a laugh."

"I will personally pay each man fifty dollars if they can pull Samson into that drainage ditch."

"Let's do it boys. Be the easiest fifty bucks we ever made." A burly farm laborer in coveralls marched over to Thompson and the other man standing by the rope on the ground. Soon more beefy challengers joined them until there were ten men standing side by side.

"Now, I want you men to pick up the rope. The last man is the anchor and needs to slip the loop around his waist," Armand said.

The men did as they were told and stood one behind the other.

Armand faced the wheat field. "Samson, time to come out!"

The tall wheat stalks parted and out stepped Samson. Much of the crowd gasped, a woman crying, "Oh my God," while an astonished man yelled, "What the hell is that thing?"

The last time Tobias had seen the Bigfoot it had been dark and he hadn't gotten a real good look at the beast. But now, even in the shrinking daylight, he could see that the creature was massive.

Standing well over eight feet tall, Samson reminded Tobias of the strongman he had once seen at the State Fair that lifted a Volkswagen Beetle over his head; only he wasn't covered with brown fur. Even under all that hair, Tobias could see Samson's Herculean pectorals and his washboard abdomen.

The muscle bound creature was bullnecked with his dome-shaped head tucked into his enormous shoulders. He had thick bulging biceps, powerful legs, and massive feet with huge toes. Tobias guessed his weight to be somewhere around 800 pounds.

Samson wore woolen trousers that ended at his shins with a rope for a belt cinched around his waist. Tobias wondered if he wore pants so as not to alarm the women.

Armand yelled. "Samson, pick up!"

Samson bent down and grabbed his end of the line with one hand.

Armand looked at the ten men. "All right, gentlemen! Get ready!"

A few of the men spit into their hands and gripped the rope tightly.

Tobias didn't see a man under two hundred pounds which didn't seem at all fair considering they outweighed the beast by over a thousand pounds.

Armand spoke to the contestants. "On the count of three I want you men to pull with all your might. One, two, THREE!"

The men lunged back a step.

Samson yowled when the rope burned through his palm. He dropped the rope and looked down, flexing his fingers.

The men almost fell backwards. "What the hell? Is he going to grab it or what?" Thompson barked.

"Forfeit," someone yelled from the crowd.

"You lose, pay up," another person shouted.

Armand shouted, "Samson! Pick up!"

Samson licked his palm. He snatched the rope off the ground and gripped it with both hands.

Armand looked at the lined-up men and then the crowd before yelling, "Now pull!"

The men grunted and tugged on the rope.

Samson took a faltering step forward.

Sensing it was an easy win, the men leaned back and pulled.

Another foot and Samson would be at the embankment.

Instead of coaching Samson, Armand watched the contest ensue.

Tobias couldn't help notice the handler grin.

Samson teetered on the edge.

"There he goes!" an onlooker yelled.

Samson gripped the ground with his toes and took a step back, shocking the men on the other side of the ditch, and halting them abruptly. Samson reached out with his right hand and yanked the rope back, extending his left hand to retrieve more line.

"Don't let him beat us!" Thompson yelled to the other men.

Each man dug his heels into the dirt but was unable to prevent being dragged forward.

Samson let out a gruff snort and quickened his hand over hand hauling method.

Thompson yelled and fell into the irrigation ditch filled with two feet of muddy water. Next came Thompson's cohort, and then a third man tumbled in. Another man dove in, followed by the one behind him, until all nine and the anchorman were stacked on top of each other like the sloppy makings of a Dagwood sandwich.

The men struggled to stand, wallowing in the mud. A few of them smiled goodheartedly when the crowd roared with laughter.

Not all of the losers shared the same sentiment. Thompson grumbled, "Damn ape should be shot for making fools of us."

Tobias figured Armand must have heard the angry comment because the handler jumped down from the platform and beckoned Samson.

The Bigfoot vaulted across the ditch in a single leap and followed Armand toward the trailers.

Tobias hoped Thompson and his crony weren't going to make trouble and figured he better warn the sheriff. But first, he thought he would swing by that stand and snag himself another one of those free delicious hotdogs.

26

THE KELPIE

Cindy and her parents were the last ones allowed inside the small-enclosed tent before the tent flaps were closed for the next showing. Twenty or so people stood behind a rope barrier, staring through the opening where the wall of canvas had been rolled up.

A man and his wife made room so the Jacobs could squeeze in and get a good view of the irrigation pond. An inverted produce crate was on the bank.

"So what are we looking at?" the man standing next to Cindy's dad asked.

"Your guess is as good as mine," her dad told the man. "All it said on the sign out front was Kelpie and no children allowed."

A dwarf wearing a red cap and a white long-sleeved shirt with a tartan sash, and a plaid Scottish kilt appeared from behind the corner of the tent and jumped up on the crate. He raised his arms and shouted excitedly, "Guid eenin! Thenk ye for coming! Me name is Duncan Doon."

A few people acknowledged the little man's greeting.

"Let me tell you all a little story," Duncan said, dropping the Gaelic for a milder Scottish accent. "Long ago, in the majestic hills near the Scottish moors, lived a beautiful lass by the name of Lola Wallace. She was a free spirit. And was loved by everyone in her village; that is everyone except for one jealous man. You see he wanted desperately to marry her. But she would have nothing to do with him, as he was a contemptible land baron and wanted only to steal her father's land. The baron decided if he couldn't have her, no one would. So he plotted to kill her.

"One sunny day, Lola ventured down to her favorite pool to bask on the rocks. While she was kneeling on the bank for a drink, the baron snuck up behind her, and pushed her head under the water."

"That's terrible," Cindy's mom said.

Duncan continued, "And when he was sure she was dead, he walked her body out to the deep end, and weighed her down with heavy stones, so she would sink to the bottom. When she didn't return, the villagers went to search for her. But she was never found. They mourn her till this day."

"What, don't tell me this is a true story?" a skeptic said from the group.

"It surely is," Duncan replied. "And no story is complete without a well-deserving ending. The baron always worried Lola's body would one day be found. When he heard the village children had discovered the pool to swim, he decided he had to retrieve the body. No one would have believed she accidentally drowned with rocks on top of her. The baron knew if she were found, the blame would point to him as everyone knew how Lola had spurned him.

"That night, he crept down to the pool. And to his disbelief, there was Lola with aquatic weeds in her hair, sitting naked on a boulder under the moonlight. How can this be? he gasped. I murdered you. Lola only smiled and dove into the pool. The baron approached the edge of the water."

Cindy noticed that everyone was enthralled by the enchanting story, especially her mother who was smiling intently, thoroughly delighted by the tale.

"Suddenly the water erupted." The dwarf threw up his arms like he was standing on a theatrical stage instead of a wooden crate.

"And a black horse emerged. The baron was caught by surprise but couldn't help wondering what had become of Lola. The horse seemed agitated so the baron reached out to calm the beast. But when he tried to remove his hand from the shiny black coat, he realized his hand was stuck like glue. The horse backed toward the deeper end and dragged the baron into the water. Just before the man went under, the horse opened its savage mouth and devoured the baron. And that is how the Kelpie came to be."

"Are you saying the woman became the horse?" a woman asked.

"That's right," Duncan answered. "A Kelpie is a shape shifting water spirit. Some say a Kelpie's purpose is to scare children away from treacherous stretches of water. Others say they guard young women from handsome scoundrels."

"So where is this...Kelpie you keeping talking about?" asked a man, shaking his head.

Duncan turned to face the pond. "Behold, Lola Wallace!"

Cindy watched with the others as a woman's head emerged slowly out of the water ten feet from the bank. But that was impossible. She would have had to have been underwater for more than ten minutes. No one could hold their breath for that long.

The woman continued to rise out of the water. Her wild shock of fiery red hair draped over her creamy white shoulders and covered her breasts. She stood, exposing her flat belly, arms resting at her sides.

"Will you look at that," a man blurted.

"Henry, keep your voice down," snapped the woman next to him.

Without saying a word, the woman in the water turned, jutted out her arms, and plunged into the pond, giving everyone a quick glimpse of her slick ivory buttocks and the bottoms of her feet.

The small splash undulated into a series of pulsating rings.

Suddenly the same spot erupted with the intensity of a natural geyser.

The Kelpie rose out of the water and stepped onto the bank.

Cindy could sense everyone's trepidation. The glistening black horse was six feet tall at the shoulders and stood with its head held high, puffing out its chest, its scraggly mane long strands of water grass. She couldn't help noticing the strange front hooves as they faced backward.

Even more disturbing was when it opened its mouth and whinnied.

Instead of tombstone teeth, the Kelpie had sharp pointy canines associated with a meat eater and not a grazer.

And then with a dramatic exit, the horse plunged into the pond, and disappeared below the surface.

"And that's our show!" Duncan Doon jumped down from the crate and disappeared behind the tent.

"Well, that was different," Cindy's mom said as they began to file out.

Scary is more like it, Cindy thought to herself.

27

POGO AND THE GNOMES

Mack convinced Anna there might still be a slight chance that Elroy could show up at the circus, claiming it was in the man's blood, like a moth unable to resist being drawn to a flame. Anna figured anything was worth a shot as they were coming up empty in the search for Suzie Fryer.

"You really think he'll show his face?" Anna said as they walked into the entrance having paid at the ticket booth.

They knew if they flashed their FBI badges they could have gotten in free, but then word might circulate and tip off their suspect if he was on the premises.

"Why not, I doubt he knows we're in Buckhorn." Mack looked through the crowd and spotted the sheriff. "Gooding's here. I imagine his wife is somewhere around."

"Best to keep our distance for now," Anna said. "If Elroy is here, we don't want him seeing us talking with the sheriff."

"Hungry?" Mack asked.

"Have you seen those lines? I am, but let's wait."

Mack walked up to a signpost in front of a tent. "Looks like there's a show about to start. Let's check it out. We can scan the audience and see if we see him."

They went inside and found seats off to the side that offered them a dim view of everyone seated around the center ring illuminated by a single spotlight.

A clown walked down the aisle carrying a large basket strapped to his waist. "Popcorn, hotdogs! Popcorn, hotdogs! Get your popcorn, hotdogs!"

"Hey, pal. Over here," Mack called out, waving to the vendor.

"What'll it be?" the clown asked. He wore a rainbow wig, bright red suspenders hiking up his baggy pants, and normal sized shoes so he wouldn't trip over his own feet.

Mack studied the man's face carefully wondering what he might look like without the makeup. He turned to Anna. "What would you like?"

"I'll take a hotdog."

"Make that two dogs and a box of popcorn," Mack told the clown. Now that he thought about it, the man was too short to be Elroy.

The clown took out two wrapped frankfurters and handed them to Mack then passed a box of popcorn. "That'll be twenty bucks."

"Twenty bucks, are you kidding?"

"They're yours now. Pal," the clown sniped, letting Mack know he didn't appreciate being called Pal.

Mack fished in his wallet and handed the clown a twenty-dollar bill.

The clown continued down the aisle like a town crier, "Popcorn, hotdogs."

Anna unwrapped her hotdog. "This sucks."

"What does?" Mack said.

"There's nothing on it."

"Jesus, you would think he'd at least given us packets of mustard and relish." Mack grabbed some popcorn and popped it in his mouth. "Think that's bad, there's no butter or salt on this popcorn."

"Oh, well. Doesn't matter. I'm too hungry to care." Anna took a bite out of her hotdog just as the spotlight beam shined down on the ringmaster in the center ring.

"Ladies and gentlemen," the ringmaster's voice bellowed over the loud speakers. "Please welcome, Pogo and the gnomes of Girona, Catalonia."

"Really," Mack said. "Gnomes?"

The announcement was acknowledged by a smattering of applause as the ringmaster stepped into the shadows and the spotlight swung over to the entranceway.

A dwarf gamboled into the middle of the ring. He had a red woolen hat with a white fluffy ball on the top of his head and a bushy white beard. He wore a blue long-sleeved shirt with large blue gloves, tan pants, and brown boots and looked like a garden gnome that had just come to life.

Mack heard groans from the audience.

"Hi, I'm Pogo," the dwarf said into the microphone in his hand. "Let me warn you, my little goblin friends can be very mischievous. The only way I can control them is with my alboka." He placed his mouth on the woodwind instrument carved from an animal horn and played a melody on the finger holes.

Thirty creatures scurried out of the dark and scampered into the audience.

"What the hell?" Mack swiveled his head to catch fleeting glimpses of the swift creatures darting about people's feet. He saw a woman raise her shoes off the floor in a panic. A man actually tried to kick one when it skittered over his boots.

He heard the mad patter of scuttling feet and people uttering quick remarks, some laughing nervously.

Mack saw a small creature snatch a box of popcorn from a little boy, spilling kernels on the floor as it ran away.

A goblin stole a cotton candy right out of a girl's hand.

A man hollered when one of them ran off with his hat.

A gnome came down Mack and Anna's row and stopped a few feet away.

Mack had never seen anything like it. It looked almost like a skinned rabbit. It had big pink hairless ears. Much of its body was pink except for blotches of green on its shoulders and steep back. The tailbone extended beyond its bulging rump making it impossible for the animal to sit on its haunches. A green muzzle covered most of its face and had two tiny pinpricks for nostril holes. It had short arms that bent at the elbows with three-fingered hands. The rear legs were long and pink with four-toed feet and resembled that of a kangaroo.

Up straight, it stood about sixteen inches tall.

"Mack, I think that's what we saw at the hotel, not a rat," Anna whispered to Mack.

"You might be right."

Mack broke off a piece of bun to offer the creature.

"Mack. What the hell are you doing? Don't feed that thing!"

The harmless looking creature eyed the morsel in Mack's hand. "Here, little buddy. It's for you." He leaned forward and his hotdog fell off his lap onto the flooring.

He went to pick it up as it was still wrapped.

The creature rose on its hind legs, hissed, and clawed Mack's hand.

"Jesus, Mack," Anna said. "I told you."

"Here you little shit, take it." Mack kicked the hotdog at the gnome. The vicious creature snatched up the food and dashed away toward the aisle.

Pogo played a melodious tune on his alboka from the center ring.

The goblins poured down the aisles like a flood of lemmings and raced out through the entranceway with Pogo right behind.

The ringmaster stepped back into the spotlight. "Let's hear it for the gnomes of Girona!" This time the applause was more robust. "Please remain in your seats and our next show, the walkaround, will begin in only a few minutes."

Mack noticed a pair of dwarf clowns in similar outfits going about the audience and returning items that the tiny creatures had stolen. The man got back his hat, the little boy was given a fresh box of popcorn, and the girl another cotton candy.

Anna was also watching the clowns. "That's nice that they do that."

"Speaking of nice." Mack glanced over at Anna's partially eaten hotdog on her lap. "I'll give you my popcorn for your hotdog."

"I don't think so." Anna gave Mack a smug grin.

"So should we stay for the next show?"

"We better," Anna replied. "It's the clown acts."

28

THE ZANIES

Tobias wandered to the rear of the big top commonly referred to as the back yard, the staging area where the performers got ready, preparing before entering the ring, when he spotted Half-Pint walking by himself. "Hey, Half-Pint, where's Penny?"

The moment the dwarf clown turned around, Tobias knew there was something different about the little man even though he was wearing the same identical costume Half-Pint wore. "The name's Dum-Dum."

"Sorry."

"No problem. I get that all the time. We do the same act."

"So when do you go on?"

"We're about to start. Come in the back door and get a good spot." Dum-Dum took off in a quick run, his short legs scissoring comically. He darted inside the tent at the same moment a horde of creatures came scampering out. They were pink and greenish and looked like hairless miniature kangaroos by the way they hopped. A dwarf with a white beard ran after them. He herded the creatures up a ramp into a canvas-covered trailer and shut the gate once the last one was inside.

He dashed back to where Tobias was standing.

The dwarf removed his hat and the bushy beard, revealing his clown face. He slipped out of his boots and took off his shirt and trousers. He wore a striped costume underneath.

"Pogo, is that you?"

"Hey, Mr. Morgan. Can't talk, running late."

Tobias watched Pogo charge inside the tent and was about to follow him when he noticed a barefoot man without a shirt wearing snug black leather pants, holding a flaming torch.

As it was almost nightfall, Tobias wondered if the man's job was to place torches around the tents.

"Do you think that's a good idea?" Tobias challenged the man.

"Hey, everybody loves danger."

Tobias noticed a large can of paraffin oil on the ground. "Aren't you afraid of burning the place down?"

"Me? No!" the man grinned. "I'm a professional. Here, I'll show you." He reached down and picked up a clear bottle filled with a taupe beige liquid, sitting next to the can. He put the neck of the bottle to his mouth and tipped the end up. He put the bottle on the ground and dabbed his mouth with a rag.

The man held the burning torch away from his face and blew out the combustible liquid like a human flamethrower creating a flaming jet of fire.

"Oh my God," Tobias said. "You're one of those fire breathers."

"That's right," the man said, scrunching his face and smacking his lips like he had a bad taste in his mouth. He extinguished the torch in a pail of water. "Would you like to see more of my act?" He grabbed a 20-inch long saber.

He leaned his head back and fed the blade down his throat into his gullet and did not stop until the hilt rested on his lips.

Tobias tried to imagine the cold steel shoved down his own windpipe and couldn't repress his own gag reflex. He put his hand over his mouth so he wouldn't distract the man. All it would take was one little nick.

The sword swallower pulled the blade out slowly and went, "Ta-da!"

Tobias stepped back "I better get inside."

"See you around," the man said, using the rag to wipe saliva off the blade.

When Tobias walked inside, the show had already commenced. He stood to the side of the arched entranceway and had an excellent view of the center ring.

Circus theme music was playing while the clowns performed their crazy antics before the audience.

Dum-Dum ran pulling the end of a long rope strung to a pulley high in the rafters, which flung Pogo high in the air, as he was tethered to the other end looped around his waist. Pogo spun around the arena, narrowly missing the people sitting in the front rows.

Each time Pogo's feet hit the ground he would take off running, only to be yanked up in the air again, causing the audience to roar with laughter.

Slappy entered the ring, driving a clown car that looked like a small delivery truck that a child might drive around the backyard. He stopped and got out, leaving the door open. A normal sized clown extracted himself from the tiny vehicle, then another crawled out, and they continued to appear.

The audience laughed louder each time a different clown came out.

Tobias counted ten clowns that had been inside the kid-sized car, parading around the perimeter of the center ring. He had no idea how they could all possibly fit inside.

Each clown went into his own routine doing pratfalls and interacting with members of the audience with sleight of the hand magical tricks.

Half-Pint was on a table performing a rola bola act, standing on a flat board and balancing on a round cylinder. He went from side to side, each time the cylinder coming mere inches from rolling off the edge of the tabletop.

Penny stood by and threw up a small bowling pin.

Half-Pint caught it. He rocked back and forth on the balancing device and snatched three more bowling pins as Penny tossed them up. Half-Pint flung each pin in the air, until he was juggling all four, and received deserving applause.

Pogo continued to spin around the center ring.

He made a large arc and flew into the dark entranceway. He disappeared for a moment then Dum-Dum yanked the end of the rope back out.

Pogo reappeared standing atop a barrel. He was propelling it forward by his shuffling feet. He entered the ring, forcing the other clowns to jump out of his way and managed a complete circle around the ring before he hopped off.

The barrel came to a stop and Patches crawled out of the open end. He tried standing but was so dizzy he couldn't stop staggering like a drunken sailor.

Patches careened into three clowns who executed theatrical pratfalls on their backsides and the house roared.

Tobias couldn't stop laughing.

He couldn't remember the last time he had so much fun and laughed this hard.

29

ODDITIES SIDESHOW

"Are you sure you want to go in?" Cindy's dad asked as he moved up in the line.

Cindy's mom looked up at the brightly lit banner over the tent entrance proclaiming ODDITIES SIDESHOW. "What could be any stranger than a pair of blue tigers and that creepy horse?"

"What's taking so long?" Cindy snapped, irritable and craving a cigarette.

Earlier, she had hoped to sneak off for a quick smoke behind the portable toilets lined up behind the tents but when she excused herself to use the restroom, her mother claimed she had to go as well and accompanied Cindy, foiling her plan. Cindy suspected her mother was suspicious and was keeping a strict eye on her even though they were supposed to be out having fun as a family.

Thankfully her mother hadn't insisted on inspecting her purse or she would have discovered Cindy's half pack of cigarettes with the Bic lighter stuffed inside.

They were directed to enter the tent with a dozen other people. Once Cindy was inside, a circus worker halted the line behind and told them to wait and they would be the next group.

Cindy had trouble seeing in the dark at first but her eyes quickly adjusted. Everyone bunched together in a narrow passage.

"Hello, everyone. I am Penny and I will be your guide."

Cindy looked over her mother's shoulder but didn't see the person talking.

"Isn't she adorable?" a woman said.

Cindy wormed her way up to the front next to her dad. She looked down and saw a short woman dressed in a child-sized dress with pink stockings and blue pumps.

"Come this way." Penny turned and started down the corridor. She marched them down to the end and made a sharp turn, cutting back so they were walking on the opposite side of the wall.

Penny stopped and stood in the center of a roped off area in front of a small stage with a black curtain drawn closed. She held a remote in her hand and pushed a button.

The curtain parted revealing a beautiful Filipino woman wearing a scanty leopard skin outfit that showed off her upper thighs and slender, tanned legs. She stood on the lighted stage behind a thick pane of glass.

"This beautiful woman's name is Belen," Penny said. "She is from the island of Mindanao in the Philippines. Belen is an Aswang."

"Hey, if all Aswangs look like that, I'm getting on the next plane," a man laughed.

Cindy saw the man pass a booze flask discreetly to another guy. She could tell by their actions they were already drunk.

"Do not be deceived by her beauty," Penny warned, lowering her high-pitched voice in a scary tone. "She's a shape shifter that can take on many forms such as a vampire, ghoul, or witch. Even though Aswangs live in the rainforest in their natural form, it is not uncommon for them to go undetected in human form, even marrying a man and later sucking the blood of the husband."

The man with the flask took a swig and shouted out. "She can—" and then the stage light suddenly flicked off casting them into darkness.

"Don't say I didn't warn you," Penny said with a little giggle.

The light snapped back on.

Cindy and her mom and the other women screamed.

"Holy shit," swore Cindy's dad.

"What the hell happened to her?" yelled one of the drunks.

The monstrous creature on the other side of the glass was something out of a nightmare. It appeared reptilian with a distinct human female anatomy. The dome of its head was smooth and it had thin slit irises in its serpentine eyes. The nose was flat and almost nonexistent except for two tiny air holes. It was the mouth that captured everyone's gaze as it was a gaping maw of jagged teeth and hung open like a yawning gator.

The Aswang snarled and flung her body at the glass.

More screams erupted as everyone jumped back.

Penny snickered and scurried down the passage. "Let's see what's on the next stage."

Afraid to be left behind with the grotesque creature, the frightened group hurried after Penny.

Cindy glanced over her shoulder and was shocked to see that the hideous Aswang had already transformed back to the beautiful Belen.

Everyone was at the next stage when Cindy caught up.

Penny opened the curtain with her remote.

A giant glass pane separated the spectators from the two diminutive humanoids standing docilely next to each other.

"These lovable creatures are Agogwes and are from eastern Africa. The male is Anesu and its partner is Chindori. They are known to live amongst large tribes of baboons though they are no way related."

Cindy studied the pair closely. Anesu and Chindori had shoulder length hair that she thought looked more like wigs. They were no taller than a couple of elementary school kids and were covered with long ginger hair that could have been bodysuits.

Neither Agogwe looked directly at the group in front of them but gazed at each other like they were enamored with one other and oblivious to their surroundings.

"They're just a couple of midgets," someone said.

"I assure you, they're real," Penny insisted. "Please, follow me."

Penny led the tour group to the next stage. She pressed her remote and the curtains opened on a strange-looking animal standing on all fours behind the glass.

"Any guess to what this is?" Penny asked.

"I've never seen such a pitiful-looking creature," a woman said.

Cindy had to admit it was rather sad to look at and reminded her of a starving mongrel on its last legs. It had a dog-like head, long neck, and rather scrawny body with gangly legs and appeared malnourished.

"This is the werewolf from the Cannock Chase Forest," Penny said.

"*The* werewolf," the drunk said. "You mean to tell me you have the only one?"

"That's right. We do."

"It doesn't look that scary to me," the other drunk said, passing the flask back to his companion.

"Don't let his looks deceive you. The Chase werewolf is a ruthless killer and can only be destroyed by a penetrating weapon made of silver."

"Doesn't look that tough to me," said the man with the flask.

"Onward and upward," Penny said, hitting the remote to close the curtain and walking down the dark corridor.

Cindy lingered for a moment as everyone followed the dwarf guide. She caught a fleeting glimpse of the creature as the curtain swiped across the glass front and almost screamed when she saw the transformed seven-foot tall werewolf standing on its hind legs, its mouth frothy with thick drool, staring down at her.

She turned and ran after the group.

"And last of all, please put your hands together for Rollo the Rubberman," Penny shouted, introducing the skinny contortionist on the stage next to a glass tank no bigger than a Plexiglas thirty-six-gallon aquarium.

Rollo smiled at his small audience. His palms were flat on the floor with his right leg bent in front of his forearms and his left leg up around the back of his neck.

He unraveled himself and lay flat on his chest with his hands on his face and his legs cocked forward so that his feet were on the top of his head in a comical pose. He stood and leaned all the way back and touched the floor with his hands. Keeping his back completely arched like his spine was a flexible strand of rubber, he went onto his elbows and cupped his hands under his chin on both sides of his face.

Cindy heard her dad say, "How in the world does he do that?"

Rollo stood and did a pantomime, pointing to the glass box.

"Don't tell me he's going to fit in that," a woman said.

Everyone watched in disbelief as Rollo lifted the glass lid and stepped inside the see-through box. He sat his butt in first then managed to squirm down so that his neck would slip inside the glass wall then his head. He raised his legs in the air and brought his right leg down first and tucked it into his chest. Then he did the same with his left leg. He wedged his right arm into his body then reached over with his left hand and closed the lid.

"That's incredible," Cindy's mom said. The group gave Rollo an earnest round of applause. He pushed open the lid and unfurled himself out of the glass box.

"And that's our sideshow," Penny said. She pulled on a rope and the tent flaps opened up.

Cindy could see the big crowd outside and thought how easy it would be to get separated from her parents and sneak a cigarette.

30

SAD HOBO

"Who are you supposed to be, Freddie the Freeloader?" snarked the clown collecting the twenty-dollar parking fee at the entrance.

"You don't like my costume?" John Paul Elroy replied and handed over the money, figuring he would be getting it back in spades.

"What the hell, the more the merrier," the clown said. "Go on through. They'll show you where to park."

Elroy nodded and drove in. He saw a man with a flashlight pointing down a long row of cars. The place was packed. This meant they were racking in the dough big time. It would be easy pickings.

He pulled the van into a vacated spot and turned off the engine.

He twisted the side mirror so he could look at his reflection.

The clown had been right. He did look like the Red Skelton character in the ruffled top hat and the sad hobo makeup. He figured someone else might make the same distinction if asked to describe him. He decided to lose the hat and tossed it on the passenger seat.

Elroy rolled the window up. He took the key out of the ignition and got out of the van. He locked the door and walked around to the rear doors. He tried listening inside the cargo area, but it was too noisy outside with the damn circus music to know if she was even awake. She was probably still out cold as he had given her a heavy sedative.

He reached inside his jacket pocket and wrapped his fingers around the handgrip of the Walther P22 wishing it was more intimidating and he had not painted it to look like a toy gun though he doubted if anyone would scoff at the silly-looking weapon if he were forced to use it.

Even though he knew nothing about this particular circus, he was familiar with the routines and the layout of the operations. He thought he would put his disguise to the test and headed toward the ticket booth. A group of young people was lined up at the window, arguing because one of the teenagers had neglected to bring enough money to pay his way.

"Jesus, Rick. I don't want to hear you forgot your wallet."

"Hey, it's true. I swear I thought I had it in my jacket."

Elroy walked up and patted the young man on the shoulder that claimed he was broke. When he turned around, Elroy reached inside his own trouser pockets and turned them inside out. He gave the man an apologetic look and shrugged like he wanted to help the young man out but he didn't have any money himself.

"Hey, get lost, Bozo," the young man snapped.

It worked like a charm. Everyone thought he was part of the circus and he waltzed right by the ticket booth. He entered the crowd and got a few looks from the children but everybody else mostly ignored him like he was part of the scenery.

He stayed clear of the main flow of foot traffic and stood by the side of a tent giving him a good view of the backdoor of the ticket booth and the rear entrance to one of the food stands.

A muscular Hawaiian man, with tribal tattoos on his bare chest and arms, stepped out from the rear of the ticket booth. He was carrying a money satchel. A black man that looked like he had been hit too many times in the face, exited the back of the concession stand, and he too, was carrying a money bag.

Elroy knew it was customary for the circus manager to have his most trusted men making hourly cash pickups at the ticket booth and the various vendor stands to minimize the cash on hand in the event of a robbery.

He noticed a stand with helium balloons for sale. He waited until the vendor was distracted with a customer and grabbed a cluster of ten.

Elroy trailed after the two men to see where they were going.

A small boy hollered. "Daddy, Daddy, I want a balloon."

"Sure son," his father said, pulling out his wallet. He stepped in front of Elroy and asked, "How much?"

Elroy could see the two men disappear into the crowd. He bared his yellow teeth at the man blocking his path. "It's your lucky day." He handed the kite strings to the man who stopped fumbling in his wallet so he could snag a couple of balloons before the rest drifted away into the night sky.

"Hey, thanks," the man said but Elroy was already rushing through the crowd.

It didn't take too long before he spotted the two couriers cutting behind a tent and heading toward the trailers.

Elroy kept to the shadows so the men wouldn't know they were being followed.

He watched the Hawaiian man go up a step and knock on a trailer door while the big black man stood and waited.

A man wearing an eye patch opened the door and beckoned the two men inside.

Elroy glanced at the luminous dial on his wristwatch.

Two more hours and they would be shutting down for the night. Time for one more money drop before he made his move.

31

NICOTINE FIX

Cindy had pretty much given up on the idea of sneaking off for a cigarette when she spotted Johnny Miles with some of his friends at a game booth. Even though Suzie and Johnny were no longer an item, Cindy knew her mother wasn't aware the couple was on the verge of breaking up and so chose to use it to her advantage.

"Mom, I just saw Johnny," Cindy said.

"Suzie's boyfriend?" her mother answered.

"Yeah, he's pretty broken up about Suzie."

Cindy saw her mother watching Johnny having fun with his friends.

"He doesn't look too upset to me."

"He's just putting on an act for his friends," Cindy assured her mother. "You know how guys are. Is it okay if I go over and talk with him? See how he's really doing."

Her mom looked to Cindy's father. He shrugged and nodded his consent.

"Okay, but don't be too long. We'll be over at the concession stand."

"Thanks Mom." Cindy turned and began walking toward the game booth. She glanced over her shoulder and saw her parents ambling to the food stand. She immediately changed direction to avoid Johnny. She always thought he was a self-absorbed jerk and had no idea what Suzie saw in him. It didn't seem to bother him that Suzie was missing.

Good riddance to you Johnny, you big creep.

Instead of going to the portable restrooms, which were on the other side of the tents, Cindy decided it would be quicker to go into the parking area for a cigarette.

She showed the man standing by the exit her ticket stub so she could re-enter the grounds. He smiled and created a short pathway of light for her with the beam of his flashlight.

A few cars were already leaving, heading down the dirt lane that would take them to the main road. Cindy stayed out of their headlights and walked between the parked vehicles. She leaned against the trunk of a Honda Civic and rummaged in her purse. She found her pack and slipped a cigarette between her lips. She held the Bic lighter at the tip of the cigarette and flicked the flint wheel with her thumb.

It sparked but no flame.

She flicked it again. Nothing.

"Shit."

"Aren't you a little young to be smoking?"

Cindy spun around. She saw a sad looking man with scraggly hair, a thin black beard, and a small red nose, with a stubby cigarette dangling out of the corner of his mouth.

She breathed a little easier when she realized he was a clown. "I'm eighteen," she told him indignantly even though she had only just turned sixteen.

"You wouldn't be fibbing to me, would you?" He took a drag of his cigarette and blew out a perfect smoke ring.

"Can I get a light?"

"I suppose." He poked his forefinger through the smoky halo. He reached into his trouser pocket and took out a Zippo lighter. He flipped the lid open and thumbed the flint wheel. A blue flame flared up. He held the lighter up to the tip of Cindy's cigarette.

As she took a puff, she could see him staring at her. Even after the tobacco was burning orange, he still held the lighter in front of her face.

"Haven't I seen you before?" he asked.

"No. I don't think so." Cindy put her purse under her arm and took a step away from the rear bumper.

The clown snapped the lid closed and extinguished the flame.

"Thanks but I have to get back to my friends," Cindy said. She thought he might think she was lying about her age—which she was—if she said she was going to meet up with her parents.

"Be seeing you." The clown turned and headed back toward the park entrance.

"I don't think so, weirdo," Cindy whispered under her breath as soon as she was certain he was far enough away and wouldn't hear her.

She was so nervous she took a deep drag hoping the nicotine would calm her nerves.

Instead she coughed.

She glanced at the cars around her. Almost all of them had the New Mexico **NM** decal stickers affixed to windshields, bumpers, or the tailgates. Some had city names like Tucumcari, Albuquerque, Mesquite, and Zuni.

Cindy spotted an old model Ford Econoline van parked a few cars away. She took a drag of her cigarette and walked toward the vehicle. She noticed the crack on the windshield on the passenger side. It looked just like the van that had been stalking them when Suzie's car ran out of gas.

She stopped and looked around to see if anyone was watching her. She saw a small family getting into their car but they were too far away to notice her.

She went up to the van, cupped her hands around her face, and peeked through the driver's side window. A banner was strewn behind the two front seats and console so she couldn't see into the cargo area. A black hat was on the passenger seat.

Cindy dropped her cigarette on the ground and squashed it with her instep.

She could smell fresh paint. And that's when it dawned on her that the van she had seen that night had been white, whereas this van was blue.

Was it possible that this could be the same one?

She took out her Bic lighter and scraped the paint on the driver's door. Blue flecks peeled off revealing a white undercoat.

"Oh my God," Cindy said. She tried the driver's door but it was locked. She went around to the passenger side and found that door locked as well. The side door too.

She moved around to the back of the vehicle. There were no windows so she couldn't see inside. She pounded on the door then put her ear up to the metal. She had to stick her finger in one ear to drown out the loud music from the circus.

She heard a bang from inside the van.

"Suzie, Suzie are you in there?" Cindy tried the handle and it moved. Either the owner had neglected to lock the door or the lock was broken. She ratcheted the handle back and forth until the door broke free from the jamb. She swung the door open and looked inside.

It was dark but she could see a person.

"Oh my God, Suzie." Cindy scrambled into the van. She crawled over to her friend who looked like she had just woken up from a coma. "Thank God, Suzie. Thank God I found you. We have to get you out of here."

She saw that Suzie's hands were bound with plastic ties. She would need to find something to cut them loose.

Suzie looked at Cindy and moaned. That's when Cindy realized that Suzie's mouth was covered with a strip of duct tape. "Here, this might hurt." Cindy grabbed one end and ripped the tape from Suzie's lips.

Suzie's eyes widened. "Cindy, behind you!"

A hand clamped over Cindy's nose and mouth forcing her to inhale the chemical on the rag.

32

PANIC

"Pete, I'm starting to get worried," Pamela Jacobs said. It had been over fifteen minutes since Cindy went off to talk with Johnny Miles and was supposed to be back and meet them at the concession stand.

"Is that the Miles boy over there?" Pete said, pointing to a group of teenagers at a shooting gallery. He slurped the last of his drink and tossed the empty cup into a waste bin.

"That's him."

Pete and Pamela marched over to confront the young man.

"So where's our daughter?" Pete asked Johnny.

"I'm sorry. I don't know what you're talking about."

"Cindy. Where's Cindy?" Pamela said.

"I don't know. Is she here?"

"What, you never saw her?" Pete said.

"No." Johnny turned to his friends and they all gave Pete and Pamela blank looks.

"Damn it, Cindy," Pamela swore and walked away.

"Honey, what is it?" Pete asked, catching up to his wife.

"She lied. She went off to sneak a cigarette."

"We don't know that."

"Come on, Pete. When are you going to stop covering for her?"

"Hey, if I do recall correctly, you gave your mother some grief when you were Cindy's age."

"That was different."

"Was it?"

Pamela took a deep breath. "Let's just find her."

"You go that way," Pete said, pointing toward the game booths, "and I'll check behind the tents. Maybe she just went to use the restroom."

Pamela held up her cell phone. "Call me if you find her."

"I will. Let's meet back here in ten minutes."

* * *

Anna and Mack were doing their best not to appear too obvious as they moved through the crowd and scanned faces for anyone that could be John Paul Elroy. Anna knew even if they did spot their suspect, he was extremely dangerous, and he wouldn't go down without a fight if they tried to make an arrest. They couldn't afford a shootout, not with all these people around.

"We'd have better luck finding a ping pong ball in a blizzard," Mack said.

"I think finding Waldo would be a better analogy." Anna sensed Mack's frustration as she was getting annoyed as well. For all she knew, their man could be hundreds of miles away and they were wasting their time; precious time that was slipping through their fingers. Chances of finding Suzie Fryer alive were dwindling faster as each day passed.

"Let's go check with the sheriff," Mack said, unable to hide the exasperation in his voice. "Elroy's not here."

"Yeah, I don't think we have to worry about blowing our cover."

It took only ten minutes to find the sheriff who was talking with a middle-aged couple. The woman seemed distraught and was almost in tears.

"Sheriff Gooding," Anna spoke as she and Mack approached.

The sheriff turned and acknowledged the agents. "This here is Pete and Pamela Jacobs."

"Oh, you must be Cindy's parents," Anna said.

"That's right," Pamela replied.

"Is there something wrong?"

"We can't find our daughter," Pete said. "We've looked everywhere."

"Could she have left with some friends?" Anna asked.

"We don't think so."

"Shelly's somewhere by the trailers, let me give her a call," Sheriff Gooding said. He keyed his two-way radio. "Shelly, we seem to have a missing girl."

"Joseph, what?" came the reply on the tiny speaker.

"No need for alarm," the sheriff said looking at the Jacobs. "I have Pete and Pamela Jacobs here and they can't find their daughter. Have you seen her?"

"No. Should I start looking?"

"Just keep an eye out."

"Will do."

"Do you have a picture of your daughter on your phone?" Anna asked Pamela.

"Yes. Give me a sec." Pamela took her phone out of her back pocket. She went through the displays until she found a good picture of her daughter's face. "Here," she said and held up her phone.

Anna took a picture of the screen from her phone.

Mack did likewise.

"I wouldn't worry," Anna said. "I'm sure she's okay. If she's here, we'll find her."

33

MONEY DROP

Andrea stretched out on the couch in the gaffer's trailer and watched Hank count the recent money drop at his desk. It always seemed to take him forever.

Maybe it was having only the one eye.

She could have sworn he'd counted the same stack of bills three times. But then she couldn't be a hundred percent sure, plagued with another one of her damn circus headaches, which were coming on more frequently, caused by being around the tigers' cages too much and breathing in the ammonia from their feces.

"Did you take something?" Hank asked, tying a large rubber band around the stack of bills.

"Yes, for the umpteenth time," Andrea said. She had her eyes closed and her forearm draped across her brow, waiting for the pain relief medication to kick in. Tonight it was a stabbing every few seconds just above her right temple.

Hank turned in his swivel chair and placed the money inside his open safe.

She knew after the last money drop, Hank would want for her to stay over in his trailer, which is why she desperately wanted to shake the headache. She had kicked off her boots and removed her vest and was wearing a thin slip top to make herself as comfortable and relaxed as possible, hoping to ease the throbbing in her head but nothing seemed to be working tonight.

She heard a knock at the door.

"That can't be Keko and Bubba already," Hank said.

Andrea listened as Hank got up from his chair.

He walked to the trailer door and opened it. She could hear the calliope music outside and Hank say, "Who the hell are you?"

"Shut up and move back," a voice snarled.

103

Andrea opened her eyes and squinted.

A man dressed like a hobo clown had entered the trailer and was pointing a toy gun at Hank who was stepping back against the front of his desk.

"Put everything in the safe in a bag," the hobo clown said.

Hank stared at the man but didn't move. "You're not one of my clowns."

"I won't ask again," the hobo clown said, jiggling his weapon to show he meant business.

"How do I know that's even real?"

Andrea saw the hobo clown do a half turn with his arm extended and point the muzzle directly at her head.

"Why don't we see," the hobo clown said and cocked the gun.

"Wait!" Hank shouted.

The hobo clown leveled the gun at Hank. "Put the money in a bag!"

Hank stepped around the desk and crouched in front of the open safe. He began transferring the money into a satchel. When the bag was completely full, he closed it up. He stood up slowly with his back turned to the robber.

"Is that all of it?"

Hank didn't answer.

Andrea's heart pounded. She knew Hank. He wasn't going to hand over the money. Too many people were depending on him.

The hobo clown was getting impatient. "Turn around nice and slow and give me the bag."

"All right," Hank said. He spun and swung the bag, knocking the gun from the hobo clown's hand. The pistol careened off the desktop and clattered between the chair and the open safe.

The hobo clown dove at Hank and they fell behind the desk.

Andrea could hear them scuffling and an exchange of hard punches.

The gunshot sounded like an abrupt crack of thunder in the trailer.

Andrea sat up and swung her feet onto the floor. Her head was splitting. She pushed herself up from the cushions and stood. "Hank?"

The hobo clown rose and came out from behind the desk.

He had possession of the gun and the bag of money.

"What have you done?" Andrea cried.

The man replied by slamming the butt of his gun into her skull.

She crumpled to the floor and the pain went away.

34

DUMB MOVE

Ernie Brown was Kenny Thompson's new drinking buddy. Kenny had made Ernie's acquaintance at the Roadside Tavern that afternoon and after sharing a couple of pitchers of beer and numerous shots—that Ernie graciously paid for—they had decided to mosey out to the Morgan farm and see what the circus was all about.

Kenny had balked at the twenty-dollar parking fee and got Ernie to cough up the money as Ernie had just cashed his monthly disability check at the bar and was proving to be a good friend to have around, at least until the well dried up.

He even convinced Ernie to pay for the both of them at the ticket booth, promising to pay him back as soon as Kenny got his paycheck, though he wasn't currently employed.

Kenny had no problem taking advantage of the gullible man. He knew if he wanted Ernie to keep footing the bill, he would have to ply Ernie with booze, which meant sharing the whiskey Kenny always toted around with him in his hip flask.

Which is what they were doing right now. Standing behind a tent, passing the flask back and forth.

The whiskey only fueled Kenny's anger. "We need to do something."

"Let it go," Ernie said, wiping his mouth and passing back the flask.

"The hell I will." Kenny stomped his boots, dislodging a few caked-on clumps. His shirt and trousers were still somewhat stiff from the dried mud. After losing the tug-a-war to the Bigfoot and being made fools of, Kenny and Ernie had gone to the pond to wash up the best they could.

"Hey, it's no big deal." Ernie leaned against the canvas and almost lost his balance. "How about we go back to that sideshow? See that Filipino woman again."

"Nobody makes a fool of Kenny Thompson, especially a Bigfoot. Wait till I get even," Kenny fumed.

"No, you're not. That's crazy talk. That thing would tie you in a knot."

Kenny downed the rest of the whiskey, tucked the flask in his back pocket, and stumbled off.

"Where're you going?" Ernie called out.

"I told you, I'm—" Kenny tripped over something in the dark and almost fell flat on his face. He turned around and looked back at Ernie. "You coming or what?"

"I don't think this is such a good idea."

"We're just going to have some fun," Kenny slurred.

"Nothing stupid, okay?"

"I'm just going to teach it a lesson." Kenny wandered toward the big rig trucks where it was dark and away from the brightly lit circus grounds.

As he and Ernie got closer, they could hear the animals pacing inside the tarpaulin-covered trailers.

Kenny approached the rear of a cage.

He reached up and grabbed a latch.

"What are you doing?" Ernie gasped.

"Going to look inside." Kenny swayed and fell against the cage.

"Are you crazy?"

"Shut your mouth." Kenny unlatched the cage door and opened it up. It was pitch-black inside.

Kenny stuck his head in and hollered, "Hey, come out and fight like a man."

"Come on, you're wasted. Let's get out of here," Ernie protested.

"Not until..." Kenny stumbled over to another flatbed trailer and fumbled open another cage. It was too dark to see anything. "Yoo-hoo!"

A menacing growl sounded from the shadows.

"We've got to go!" Ernie grabbed Kenny by the sleeve.

"Hey!" Kenny pulled away. He staggered over to two more enclosures and opened the cage doors.

Ernie stayed on Kenny's heels. "Will you stop? Ah man, that smell." Ernie covered his nose.

"Holy shit," Kenny said. "What took a crap in here?"

"Hey, you guys can't be back here," shouted a short man dressed like a garden gnome.

Kenny laughed at the dwarf. "And who says?"

A giant creature leaped out of a cage.

It looked like a massive wolf standing on its hind legs. It grabbed Ernie by the shoulders and hoisted the screaming man off of his feet.

Kenny watched in horror as the creature shoved Ernie's head into its mouth and crunched down on his skull. Seashell-sized pieces of cranial bone and globule brain slopped onto the ground.

"Jesus," Kenny screamed. He turned to run and slammed into the dwarf, knocking him to the ground.

The beast straddled Ernie's body. It raised its right paw and plunged its razor-sharp talons deep inside Ernie's chest and ripped out his ribcage full of organs in a colossal blood-smattering mess.

Kenny saw the dwarf get up and take off running as he too turned tail and ran for his life.

35

OFF TARGET

Half-Pint, Penny, and their son, Patches, were on their way to their trailer when they saw a hobo clown walking through the crowd, carrying a satchel.

"Who's that?" Penny asked.

"I don't know," Half-Pint replied.

"Isn't that one of the gaffer's bags?" Patches said.

"I think it is."

"I thought only Keko and Bubba made money drops," Penny said.

"You're right. You and Patches go tell the gaffer. I'm going to follow this guy."

"You be careful." Penny gave her husband a quick kiss.

"Hurry," Half-Pint said and went after the hobo clown.

Penny and Patches dashed over to the trailers. When they reached the gaffer's quarters, Penny hopped up the steps and rapped on the door.

"No one's answering?" Patches said, waiting at the foot of the steps.

"That's odd." Penny turned the knob and pulled open the door. She saw Hank's feet sticking out from behind the desk and Andrea sprawled on the floor next to the couch. "Oh my God," she yelled. She turned to her son. "Go get Doc, now!"

Patches took off running to fetch the circus physician.

Penny rushed over to Andrea who had a nasty gash on her forehead. The tiger handler's eyes were closed. Penny grabbed a pillow from the couch and when she put pressure on the head wound to staunch the bleeding, Andrea let out a groan. Penny jumped up to take a look at her boss.

Hank was unconscious. He looked like he had either been shot or stabbed, as the belly of his shirt was soaked with blood. His chest heaved slightly.

"Thank God, you're both alive," Penny said.

She glanced at the open safe and saw that it was empty.

That's when the realization hit her; they'd been robbed!

Penny heard Andrea moan. She went over and knelt by her side. "Andrea, don't worry, help is on the way. Who did this to you?"

Andrea opened her mouth to speak but nothing came out.

"Was it the hobo clown?" Penny asked.

Andrea answered with a nod.

"Oh my God," Penny said. Half-Pint was going after a madman.

* * *

Half-Pint stayed a safe distance behind the hobo clown but never let him out of his sight. He kept looking around hoping to see Keko or Bubba and get their attention but they were nowhere to be seen. It was obvious the man Half-Pint was following was doing his best to avoid any of the circus crew as they might have stopped to question who he was as everyone knew everybody that worked for the outfit.

The hobo clown cut back behind a game booth and headed for the back yard behind the big top.

Half-Pint scurried after him.

It was rather dark behind the giant canopy, and for a moment, Half-Pint thought he had lost him. But then the man appeared from out of the shadows where Magnus and Lady McBeth were standing near the rear entrance waiting to go inside the big top for their last performance for the night.

Armand stepped out of the circus tent. Samson lumbered out behind his handler.

Half-Pint rushed over. "Armand, I need your help."

Armand stopped and turned. "Hey, Half-Pint, what's up?"

"See that guy over there?" Half-Pint pointed to the figure walking toward Magnus and Lady McBeth.

"Yeah, what about him?"

"Do you know who he is?"

"Nope, never saw him before. Why?"

"I think he stole one of the money drop bags."

"What?" Armand said.

"We have to stop him," Half-Pint said.

Armand looked up at Samson. "Come on, big guy."

Half-Pint followed behind the handler and his Bigfoot.

"Hey, buddy," Armand called out to the stranger. "Hold up for a second."

The hobo clown spun around and pulled a toy gun out of his pocket. "Stay back."

Samson glared at the puny weapon and snarled. The muscle-bound creature took a step forward. Armand grabbed the waistband of Samson's short trousers. "Not yet."

"What's going on?" Magnus said and turned in the direction of the voices.

The hobo clown stepped behind Lady McBeth and threw his arm around her waist, still managing to hold onto the satchel. He put the muzzle of the gun up to her head. "Take one more step and she's dead."

Everyone froze.

"What's happening?" Magnus jerked his head back and forth.

"He's got Lady McBeth!" Half-Pint yelled.

"Magnus!" Lady McBeth shouted in alarm.

The blind knife thrower snatched a blade from his belt.

The hobo clown pocketed the gun and clamped his hand over Lady McBeth's mouth. "Well, if it isn't Jim Bowie."

"Who are you?" Magnus growled.

"I'm the one holding a gun to your lady friend's head."

"Don't listen to him," Half-Pint yelled. "He's trying to trick you."

Magnus cocked his head in the direction of the man holding Lady McBeth hostage.

"What are you waiting for?" the hobo clown taunted.

Magnus flung the knife underhanded at the man's voice.

The blade struck with a soft thud.

The hobo clown released Lady McBeth and she collapsed to the ground with the knife handle sticking out of her chest.

"No!" Half-Pint screamed.

Armand and the Bigfoot ran toward the fallen body as the hobo clown backed away.

"Samson, get the son of a bitch," Armand said and the Bigfoot stomped toward the man.

The hobo clown spotted three torches soaking in a fire breather's bucket of paraffin oil. Instead of pulling out his gun, he dropped the satchel, and took out a cigarette lighter. He grabbed the sticks with the combustible balls of gauze on the ends and ignited them with his lighter.

Samson stopped when he saw the burning torches.

The hobo clown tossed a torch at the Bigfoot, which struck his leg and set his hair on fire. Armand went to help Samson but the frightened Sasquatch was already running back inside the big top.

The man turned and threw the remaining two torches at the backside of the big top. Two separate fires licked up the canvas and quickly merged into one gigantic blaze.

The hobo clown took advantage of the diversion, grabbed the satchel, and ran off.

Half-Pint gazed up at the raging fire and the billowing clouds of smoke spiraling into the night sky. People were already screaming inside.

36

MAYHEM

It was a mass exodus coming out of the big top. People screamed and fell over one another as they scrambled for safety. Parents carrying their children collided with others jostling to get out. It was everyone for themselves.

Half-Pint was mowed over and knocked to the ground. He got on his knees and bent forward, clasping his hands together over his head. He got kicked in the ribs and someone used his back as a springboard to escape the fire.

Armand ran over to Magnus kneeling beside Lady McBeth. He put his hand on her neck and felt a pulse. "We have to get out of here," Armand yelled. "The place is on fire." Armand scooped Lady McBeth up in his arms. "Grab my belt," he yelled. Magnus held on and they scurried away from the inferno.

Samson came running out of the blazing tent, his entire body hair singed and blackened and fled with the others like an elephant running in the middle of a stampeding antelope herd.

The fire engulfed the big top. Large strips of burning canvas rose in the air under the belching heat, along with flying embers.

It took only the span of a minute before the concession stands' rooftops and some of the other tents had caught fire.

Sheriff Gooding yelled into his cell phone. "Get the auxiliary over here quick! We got ourselves a fire! What? What do you mean all the volunteers are gone? Don't tell me they're here! Damn it! Then send the truck! And ambulances!" He ended the call and looked at Pete and Pamela Jacobs. "Cindy will have to wait. I've got to make sure everyone gets out of here safe."

"We understand, Sheriff," Pete said.

"Look out," Pamela yelled.

Fifty people stampeded straight for them.

Near the ticket booth, Shelly tried to get everyone to leave in an orderly fashion but they were too scared to listen to her and raced by. She had to step back or be trampled. A woman flew past her and was struck from behind by a large man. She went sprawling to the ground. Shelly rushed over, grabbed the woman's hand, and dragged her out of the path of the maddening rush.

Anna and Mack went looking for anyone injured. They found an unconscious teenager lying on the ground. Mack picked the boy up and threw him over his shoulder in a fireman's carry. "I'll take him to the parking area away from the fire."

"Good. I'll go find Meyers," Anna said. She turned and ran toward the trailers.

Rocky Hardman had gotten some of his roustabouts combating the flames thanks to Tobias' ingenuity. A large trestle on wheels equipped with hundreds of irrigation sprinkler heads Tobias used for his fields was pumping water from the pond and spraying the base of the burning big top.

Anna reached Hank Meyers' trailer and saw that the door was standing open. She hurried up the steps and saw a man in a white coat kneeling by the desk. A female dwarf in a clown costume was sitting on the couch next to a woman holding her head and a dwarf boy wearing a costume with patches on his shirt and pants.

"What's going on?" Anna asked. "You guys really need to get out of here. The place is on fire."

"What? Who are you?" asked the female dwarf.

"I'm Special Agent Rivers with the FBI. Who are you?"

"I'm Penny. This here's Andrea."

"I caught part of her show. The big cats, right?"

"That's right," Penny said. "The boy's my son, Patches." Penny jumped off the couch and stepped over to the door. "Oh my, there're flames everywhere."

"How are you doing, Andrea?" Anna asked.

"Bastard walloped me good," Andrea replied.

"Who did?"

"The hobo clown," Penny said, looking back inside. "He took our money and shot Hank."

"What? When was this?"

"Ten, fifteen minutes ago."

Anna reached in her pants pocket and took out her phone. She speed-dialed her partner. "Mack, are you still at the parking area?"

"Yeah, where are you?"

"There's been a robbery. Look for a hobo clown."

"And he has a money drop bag," Penny added.

"He'll be carrying a bag," Anna said into the phone.

"Gotcha," Mack replied.

"Mr. Meyers, Mr. Meyers," a high-pitched voice hollered outside the door.

Anna turned and saw a dwarf dressed like a garden gnome scamper up the steps.

"Pogo, what's wrong?" Penny asked.

"We're in big trouble."

"We know. The fire. We're going to leave as soon as we can move the boss."

"No, you don't understand. Some jerks opened the cages."

"Who did?" Andrea asked.

"Some gillies. One's dead."

"What's a gilly?" Anna asked.

"Someone not associated with the circus," Andrea said. "Pogo, what about my tigers?"

"They're gone."

"Aren't tigers renowned man-eaters?" Anna said.

"Not mine. They're gentle as housecats as long as I'm with them and they're not provoked."

"But what if you're not and they feel threatened?"

"I don't think the tigers killed him," Pogo said.

"Why's that?" Anna asked.

"I think it was the werewolf."

"Oh my God," Andrea said. "You mean they all escaped?"

"That's right."

"What does this mean?" Anna asked.

"It means all hell is about to break loose," Andrea said.

37

ESCAPE ARTISTS

Suzie heard screaming voices and loud car engines outside. She shouted, "Help! We're in here! Help!" but she knew no one was going to hear her from inside the van with all the chaotic noise out there. She used her bound feet and nudged her friend lying on her side with her hands tied behind her back. "Cindy, wake up!"

Cindy's mouth was covered with duct tape. She groaned and her eyes flickered open for a second.

"Come on, snap out of it." Suzie could smell the faint odor of chloroform from the rag lying on the cargo floor.

After the kidnapper had rendered Cindy unconscious, he first secured Cindy's wrists together with zip ties and then her ankles. Afraid someone might walk by and see the girls tied up in the back of the van, their abductor had hastily slapped tape over Cindy and Suzie's mouth and shut the rear door.

It took her awhile, but finally Suzie was able to peel the tape off by rubbing her mouth against her shoulder.

A speeding vehicle barreled by outside and shook the van.

"Come on, Cindy!"

Cindy opened her eyes. She looked like she was waking up with the worst hangover in her life.

"Scoot over here and get on your knees," Suzie said, unable to move as her hands were bound to the van's metal wall.

Cindy wormed over to Suzie's feet and managed to get up on her knees.

"Get closer."

As her friend leaned in, Suzie was able to sink her teeth on the end of the tape covering Cindy's mouth. She turned her head and pulled the tape off.

"Jesus, Suzie. I thought I would never see you again."

"Am I glad to see you."

"Why is he doing this?"

"I don't know. Where are we? How did you find me?"

"We're at some dumb circus," Cindy said.

Outside, engines revved and peopled screamed.

"What's going on out there?" Suzie said.

"I have no idea."

"Do you think you could get free?"

"Maybe." Cindy tried to stretch the plastic ties binding her wrists together. "He didn't tighten them all the way." She stretched her arms down and worked her hands under her rump. It was a struggle but soon she had her hands under her thighs. She bent her legs and pulled her hands out in front of her.

"Look for something sharp," Suzie said.

Cindy looked through the crates filled with clown apparel. She opened a small toolbox with cartoon animal stickers and took out a rusty carving knife. She tucked the handle between her ankles with the blade up and began sawing away at the plastic ties cinching her wrists. The blade was dull but finally it cut through. Cindy rubbed her wrists. She took the knife and freed her feet.

"Hurry," Suzie said.

Cindy sliced through Suzie's restraints and saw that Suzie was only wearing a rumpled T-shirt. "Where're your clothes?"

"I don't know. We need to get out of here." Suzie scrambled to the front of the dark cargo hold, thinking they could crawl out through the cab. All she would have to do is tear down that banner. But when she went to grab it, her fingers struck a wire mesh screen. She grabbed it with both hands and shook it but it was a thick gauge and proved solid.

"We can get out the back," Cindy said. "I don't think the lock works very well. If I can give it few good kicks, I can get it open." She slid over to the double doors. She raised her knees and gave a door a violent kick with both feet.

"Do it again!" Suzie yelled.

Cindy brought her legs back.

The van rocked forward with a big boom and the rear doors buckled inward.

"What just happened?" Cindy said, crawling toward Suzie.

An engine roared and tires pealed in the dirt.

"Someone just hit us."

Cindy scooted over to inspect the doors. "They're wedged shut. We're trapped."

Men were yelling outside.

They heard the van door on the driver side open then slam shut.

"Oh my God, he's back," Suzie said.

The engine started up and the van lurched forward in a tight turn, tossing Suzie and Cindy about in the back.

They heard a loud ping ricochet off the side of the van.

"Jesus, Suzie," Cindy screamed. "Someone's shooting at us."

38

DEMOLITION DERBY

As soon as Mack heard the teenager groan, he stopped and slipped him off of his shoulder. He sat him down and propped the boy against the sidewall of the ticket booth.

"How's your head?" Mack asked, examining the bump on the boy's forehead.

"It hurts."

"Yeah, I bet it does. That's quite a goose egg." Mack spotted Shelly who was helping a battered woman. "Deputy Gooding!"

Shelley looked over.

"Can you see he gets medical attention when the ambulances arrive?"

"Sure."

"Have you seen our suspect?"

"He may have snuck past, I don't know."

Another group of hysterical people charged by. A man went sprawling like a baseball player sliding headfirst into the home plate. Two screaming women used him for a stationary treadmill and fled into the parking area.

Mack watched cars and trucks pulling out of the parking slots, speeding in all directions without any regard for the people running hysterically between the vehicles.

He saw a woman get struck by a compact sedan and get scooped up in the air. She struck the top of the windshield, flew over the roof, hit the lid of the trunk, and rolled onto the ground in the path of a fast-moving pick-up truck with its headlights off.

The left front all-terrain tire ran over her head, squashing it flat like a pancake as the right front tire busted her legs into kindling. The rear tires did more of the same.

He witnessed cars smashing into each other; some minor fender benders as they kept going; others wrecked and refusing to start.

Mack heard men yelling and looked back at the burning tents. A section of the big top had collapsed and sent the ceiling pole and much of the rigging crashing to the ground, trapping people underneath the burning wreckage.

Roustabouts were struggling to lift the fallen debris off the screaming victims.

A charred-looking creature stepped out of the swirling smoke and stomped over to the rescuers. It was Samson the Bigfoot. He was black from head to toe and looked like he had rolled around in a coal bin.

The men made room for Samson. He grabbed the heavy pole like a weightlifter and curled the heavy stanchion up to his chest allowing the men to extricate the injured.

Mack heard the loud impact of smashing metal and turned to the sound of the crash and spotted the hobo clown with the satchel, darting between the cars.

"Deputy Gooding," Mack hollered but the officer was preoccupied helping a young girl that was crying. "Shelly!" he persisted.

She looked over at him.

Mack pointed at the fleeing man. "Do you see him?"

Shelly gazed out at the carnage. "Yes. He's getting into a van."

"Call your husband. I'm going after him." Mack took off and sprinted into the bedlam. He kept glancing at the van but had to look away fast when a car sped toward him. He jumped out of the way and was clipped on the elbow by the driver side mirror.

The van backed up and made a half turn.

Mack stopped and drew his sidearm.

He could see the hobo clown behind the wheel.

Suddenly, the van lurched and raced straight for him.

Mack raised his pistol, lined up the driver in his sights, and pulled the trigger just as the van swerved. He heard the bullet strike the side of the van.

He dove out of the path of the speeding vehicle and ended up in the dirt. He sat up quickly and saw the fleeing taillights fading down the property. He got to his feet just as a car came to a skidding halt beside him.

"Get in," Sheriff Gooding yelled from behind the wheel.

Mack jumped into the police cruiser.

"We've got the bastard now," the sheriff growled and tromped on the accelerator.

39

NIGHTMARE FIELD

"You better show me the body," Anna told Pogo.

"Right this way, lady."

"I'm going with you," Penny said and began to follow Anna down the steps.

Patches went to join his mother. "I want to come."

"That might not be such a good idea," Pogo said glancing up at Penny.

"He's right. You better stay here and help Andrea."

"But Mom..."

A dwarf in a filthy clown suit ran up.

"Hey Dad," Patches said.

"So what happened?" Half-Pint asked.

"You were right to be suspicious," Penny said. "We were robbed. He hurt Mr. Meyers and Andrea."

"I knew it. Where are you guys going?"

"Pogo has something to show us," Penny replied.

"Who are you?" Half-Pint asked Anna.

"She's with the FBI," Penny answered for the agent.

Patches gave his father a pleading look. "Can I go?"

Half-Pint turned to Penny. She shook her head.

"Sorry, son. Not this time."

Anna and the three dwarfs took off running down between the trailers and the big rig trucks, stopping short of the flatbeds that hauled the covered cages. Even in the gloom of night, Anna could see the cage doors standing open.

They walked slowly over to the body lying on the ground.

"Oh my God," Penny gasped when she saw the ravaged man with the hollowed-out chest cavity in the middle of a sloppy circle of strewn entrails.

"And you think the werewolf did this?" Anna asked.

"I'm sure of it," Pogo said, and pointed up at the enclosure. "That's its cage."

"Let's go hunt it down," Half-Pint said. He went around to the side of the trailer and opened a long metal box attached to the bed. He reached inside and grabbed a spear with a sharp point. He wielded the weapon and the tip glinted in the faint moonlight.

Two short figures rushed over.

"Slappy, Dum-Dum, you're just in time," Half-Pint said. "Grab a spear, we're going werewolf hunting."

The five dwarfs looked like a pigmy tribe of warriors armed with their spears.

"Maybe it would be better if I handled this," Anna said showing the dwarfs her service pistol strapped to her hip.

"Sorry, lady, that won't—" Half-Pint stopped when he heard a woman scream.

"Where did that come from?" Penny asked.

Anna ran to a spot where she could see beyond the trailers. She saw a large clearing and the six-foot tall wall of wheat field.

Two people dashed into the dense crop. She could see their heads only for a moment before they disappeared into the dark.

A large animal loped on all fours across the clearing in pursuit and charged in after them.

"I think I saw it." Anna rushed out into the clearing. She glanced over her shoulder and saw the five dwarfs running as fast as their short legs could carry them in order to keep up.

Anna took her flashlight out of her coat pocket. She turned it on as she drew her gun and bolted into the stalks of wheat.

She heard the woman scream again but this time it was higher pitched. A man's yell was accompanied by a savage howl.

The dwarfs were somewhere behind her, lost in the tall wheat.

Anna shined her light on the ground and followed a path of flattened wheat stalks until she reached a dirt path clearing. She caught a glimpse of the man and woman running in the direction of the burning flames.

A noise caused her to spin around.

She pointed her gun, halting at the sight of an emaciated creature that resembled a large lazy greyhound with a flat snout and pointy ears, lying in the dirt. It was licking its front paws and paid her no mind as if she wasn't there.

It seemed inconceivable that this submissive animal could possibly be dangerous.

The creature lifted its chin and stared into her eyes.

Anna felt compelled to lower her gun.

The creature rose off its belly and stood on its hind legs.

Anna watched helplessly as it towered over her, the bones in its body elongating while its muscles squared out its shoulders and puffed out its chest. The snout enlarged and extended revealing vicious fangs and a mouthful of savage teeth.

The werewolf grabbed her by the shoulders with its clawed paws and yanked her off her feet. She managed to raise the muzzle of her gun and fired three shots into the beast's chest.

Never once did it flinch.

It squeezed her like a compressing vise.

Her gun slipped from her fingers. She stared into the gaping maw.

The monster opened its jaws wide...

"No you don't!" came a voice from behind.

The werewolf yowled and released Anna.

She could hear grunts and jabbing sounds.

The creature flailed and gasped as it went into anaphylactic shock.

It collapsed on the ground, impaled with five spears, and jerked about until finally it let out a whimper and reverted back to its tame-looking self and became still.

Sitting in the dirt, Anna felt her head clearing as if she had been under a trance.

She looked up and saw the five dwarfs standing around her.

"I tried to tell you, only one thing affects a werewolf," Half-Pint said triumphantly and pulled a spear out of the werewolf's body. He held up the shaft with blood dripping off the tip. "Silver."

"Then it's dead?" Anna asked.

"Oh, yeah. It's dead all right," Penny said.

"Five times dead," Pogo piped in as Slappy and Dum-Dum whooped a cheer.

40

BATHING BEAUTY

Camden had a majestic view from the guard shack of the 402 homes below and the town lights of Buckhorn. He saw a distant glow on the horizon and could not imagine what it could be. He thought he heard sirens but was not completely sure. The desert could play tricks on the imagination, especially at night.

Camden reviewed his logbook and made a notation that he would have to give a warning slip to one of the residents when he stopped at the guard shack as the Desert Sands Estates Homeowner Association was citing the person for excessive use of his water sprinkler system as it was leaving heavy runoff on the street.

He prepared a visitor pass for a repairman scheduled to come an hour before Camden's shift was up with a work order to fix a faulty garage door that refused to close as the roller spring had broken on an unoccupied house that was currently on the market.

Everything seemed quiet so he pulled out a *National Geographic* from the cubby and sat in the chair. He opened the cover and flipped through the pages until he found an article about Greenland and the people that lived there. He was a paragraph in when he heard galloping hooves.

Camden looked up and saw a dark shadow flash by the window. It was too bright inside the guard shack for him to see what it was through the window.

He stood, tossed the magazine on the chair, and took a step outside through the side door. He expected to see a stray cow that had gotten out of its pasture or a renegade mustang that had lost its way running down the street. He saw no such thing under the streetlamps.

He shook his head and sat back down with his magazine.

A minute later, he heard what sounded like a herd of small animals racing by the kiosk. He popped out of his chair and stepped outside.

Again, there was nothing.

"I must be losing it," he muttered to himself.

He went inside and sat back down. He was reading about the Norsemen and how Leif Ericson was believed to be the first European to reach North America—500 years before Christopher Columbus made his claim—when a series of car alarms went off.

"What now?" He grabbed the keys to the golf cart off the hook and was about to step out when a van doing thirty—fifteen miles an hour over the posted speed limit within the community—sped by forcing him to dive out of the way or he would have been run over. "Hey! What the hell!"

He was getting to his feet when he heard the quick whoop of a police siren.

Sheriff Gooding pulled up in his cruiser. A man sat in the front passenger seat.

The sheriff lowered his window and looked up at Camden. "Are you okay?"

"Yeah," Camden replied.

"Did you see which way that van went?" the sheriff asked.

Camden turned and looked at the turnaround that split off into three separate streets leading into the community but didn't see any taillights. "I'm not sure? Who was it?"

"We're pretty sure it's the guy that kidnapped Suzie."

"Shit, Sheriff. Take me with you and I'll help you find them."

"No, you better stay here. Just in case he doubles back."

The sheriff sped off before Camden could say another word.

"The hell with this." Camden locked the guard shack and jumped into the golf cart.

* * *

Bernard Campbell had a bad habit of falling asleep in front of the television and tonight had been no exception. He woke up to the sound of cars racing outside and blaring car alarms. He got up from his La-Z-Boy recliner and turned off the set. The digital clock on the mantel read 11:13. His wife and two girls had long since gone to bed.

He debated whether to go out front and see what all the commotion was about but then the alarms subsided and it was quiet again.

Bernard did what he did every night before retiring and went around making sure all the downstairs' windows and doors were locked. He checked the back sliding glass door and was about to close the drapes when he saw that something had triggered the automatic motion detector spotlight over the backyard swimming pool.

The pool was his pride and joy. He had spent a fortune turning his backyard into a natural lagoon surrounded by cultured rock with a waterfall that circulated the crystal clear water.

A naked woman sat seductively on the stonework at the base of the cascading water splashing down onto the swimming pool's surface. She had pale skin and long red hair that draped over her bosom.

Bernard glanced over his shoulder to make sure his wife was not there though he knew her to be a sound sleeper. He felt guilty watching another woman, especially one without any clothes. He watched the voluptuous creature on the rock. She reminded him of a siren that would lure unwary sailors.

She was cupping water from the pool and letting it run down her body.

He reached down and opened the sliding glass door. He stepped out onto the concrete in his slippers, his robe dangling open with the hanging sash.

"Hello?"

The woman appeared not to hear him. She splashed more water on herself.

"I don't think we've met," Bernard said, keeping his voice low so as not to wake anyone in the house.

He figured she must be one of his neighbors from behind and had hopped over the fence. He prayed she wasn't drunk. That's all he needed was for someone to drown in his pool and get sued for everything he owned.

"Maybe you should leave." He was almost to the edge of the pool.

The woman continued to pamper herself.

"No, seriously, I think—" but before he could finish, the woman dove headlong into the pool.

Bernard kicked off his slippers and tore off his robe, ready to jump in after her before she ended up drowning.

He put his arms up in preparation to dive in.

A black horse with glowing eyes and mouth full of sharp serrated teeth burst out of the water.

Bernard's scream was cut short when the horse bit off his head.

41

SEEING DOUBLE

Mark Taylor was much too excited to sleep.

His duffle with all his hunting gear and his suitcase of clothes were sitting by the front door along with his gun bag packed with plenty of ammunition and his hunting rifle.

He had arranged for an Uber driver to pick him up at five in the morning and take him to a private airport where a charter plane would be waiting to fly him and his buddies up for a five-day stay at their favorite hunting lodge.

He paced his three-bedroom home, admiring his hunting trophies throughout his house.

A massive elk head with a giant rack was mounted over the fireplace in the living room; a long-tusked boar's bust hung in his den; a twelve-point stag was on the wall in the guest bedroom; a curled-horned ram stared blankly with glass eyes from the master bedroom wall.

Mark went to his wet bar and poured himself a stiff scotch without ice. Taking a gulp, he stared pensively at the array of taxidermy displayed about the room.

He walked over with his drink and stood at the sliding glass door, ruminating about the possibilities of his trip. He glanced through the glass and went, "Holy shit!" He couldn't believe his eyes.

An enormous tiger was drinking from his swimming pool. He wondered where it had come from then remembered his neighbors making a big fuss about the circus that was just outside of town. Somehow this animal must have escaped and jumped the fence into his backyard.

Mark thought of picking up the phone and calling the sheriff but decided to wait.

He sipped his scotch and watched the big cat drink from the pool.

It looked like a giant Bengal and was blue with dark stripes. He figured it must weigh well over a thousand pounds. He imagined how great it would be to have the thing rendered lifelike in his living room.

Sure the taxidermist would charge him a fortune—and would have to be discreet—but think what his buddies would say. They'd shit their pants.

Mark glanced over at his gun bag next to the travel cases by the front door. He looked back at the magnificent beast. He made up his mind and polished off his drink.

Placing the glass down on an end table, he marched over to the front door. He unzipped his gun bag and pulled out his hunting rifle. He grabbed a five-shot magazine, popped it in, and slid back the bolt, ramming a cartridge into the chamber.

He went over to the sliding glass door, carrying his rifle in the crook of his arm. He opened the door quietly so as not to spook the animal. The tiger continued to lap up the water with its huge tongue.

Mark stepped out on the patio. He crept toward the beast. He put the gunstock against his shoulder, pointed the barrel, and stared into the high-power scope.

He lined up where he estimated the tiger's heart to be in the middle of the crosshairs then eased his finger on the trigger, ready to pull...

Mark heard a loud huff behind him. He turned his head slowly.

And came face to face with a tiger standing only five feet away that was even bigger than the one drinking from the pool. He could feel its hot breath on his face.

"Ah, easy there," Mark said, doing his best to remain calm even though the only thing he wanted to do was run like hell back inside his house.

The tiger kept staring at Mark.

"Hey, everything's cool," Mark said, lowering the rifle slightly so that it was no longer pointing directly at the other animal. He tried not to show any sign of fear, thinking the big cat would smell it on him and attack. He kept his finger poised over the trigger ready to swing the rifle around and shoot.

Mark's left arm was grabbed from behind and yanked backward.

The tiger that had been drinking from the pool had snuck up on him. It had half his arm in its mouth. The jagged teeth clamped down and bit deep into the bone.

"Jesus—" he screamed and raised the gun muzzle.

The other tiger seized his right arm in its mouth, forcing him to drop the rifle.

"No, no, no..."

The tigers toyed with him and pulled on his arms like they were playing a mischievous game of tug-a-war.

"Please, don't," Mark pleaded.

The big cats stepped back, ripping Mark's arms from his shoulders like he was made of straw. Blood spurted from the sockets, hosing the patio.

He fell to his knees, screaming as the tigers made a quick meal of his arms.

They ambled back and each grabbed a leg.

Mark blacked out when they snapped his pelvis like a wishbone.

42

NO PLACE LIKE GNOMES

"Seriously, you never saw this movie?" Tim Sykes asked his girlfriend, Lynne Dillard, as they sat on the couch watching *Gremlins*. They had spent the day at the circus and were staying up late at Lynne's house to watch scary movies while her parents visited the circus.

Tim and Lynne were at the part of the movie when Billy Peltzer's mother discovered the *mogwai* cocoons in Billy's room and was coming downstairs to investigate a noise she heard coming from the kitchen.

"No, I told you—"

Something smashed in the kitchen.

"What was that?" Lynne gasped.

Tim picked up the remote and paused the movie. "What? I didn't hear anything."

Another crash sounded in the kitchen.

"There. Did you hear it?"

Tim stood and gazed across the room. "Sure it's not your cat?"

"Luna's over there."

Tim spotted the tabby on the chair by the fireplace. It must have heard the noise because it hissed and arched its back.

"Go see what it is," Lynne said.

"Are you crazy?"

"Then call 9-1-1. Where's your phone?"

Tim reached in his pocket. "Damn, I left it in the kitchen."

"Wait a minute," Lynne said and scowled at Tim. "Are you pranking me?"

"What do you mean?"

"You set something up on your phone. Didn't you?"

"No, I swear. There's something in the kitchen."

Lynne looked at the image on the TV screen of Mrs. Peltzer peering around the corner at a gremlin eating out of her electric mixing bowl. "Yeah, perfect timing."

"No, I'm not kidding."

"Enough already." Lynne slipped her feet off the couch and was about to get up when a strange creature scampered into the room. She screamed, plopped back on the couch, and clutched a pillow to her chest.

The thing looked like a cross between a hairless rabbit with big pointy ears and a miniature kangaroo with large feet. It was mostly pink with specks of green like someone had flicked paint at it.

"Holy shit, it's one of those gnomes from the circus," Tim said. "What's it doing here?"

"It's creepy. Get it out of here," Lynne said.

Luna hissed from the chair.

Tim studied the creature. "Somehow this one looks different from the ones we saw at the circus."

"It does," Lynne said. "Weren't they wearing some kind of mask?"

The gnome curled its upper lip and showed off its savage teeth.

Tim couldn't take his eyes off the creature. "No, I think they were muzzles."

"So what happened to this one's?" Lynne asked with a trembling voice.

The gnome suddenly launched itself across the room. It landed on the chair by the fireplace. Luna jumped up on the headrest. She hissed and swiped her claws.

The creature hopped up to snare the cat but Luna was too fast and leaped onto the floor. She dashed across the room and jumped into Lynne's lap.

The gnome hit the floor and with one bound, landed on the coffee table, knocking the glass bowl of popcorn on the floor.

Tim snatched the decorative glass dish and smacked the gnome in the face. The creature fell back and toppled off the coffee table.

Lynne held Luna and jumped up so Tim could wrap his arms around her.

"Whoa, it's okay," Tim said. "I think I killed it."

"Thank God." Lynne could not stop shaking.

Tim looked down at the creature on the floor. The glass dish had caved in most of the gnome's face. "See, there's nothing to worry about."

A drawer spilled open in the kitchen, clattering silverware.

"What was that?" Lynne said.

Tim and Lynne turned to the kitchen.

Ten gnomes crowded in the doorway, staring at the goblin lying dead on the carpet. None were wearing muzzles.

"Don't panic," Tim whispered. "Move slowly."

Tim and Lynne took single steps backwards.

The cat fussed in Lynne arms, raising its hackles and hissed.

"Luna, shush," Lynne hissed back.

The gnomes screeched and charged into the living room.

43

RUMP ROAST

Mack stared out his window while the sheriff panned his spotlight on the vehicles parked on the other side of the street. They had canvassed a large part of the neighborhood but so far had not found the van.

"Looks like he pulled a Houdini," Mack said.

"He's got to be somewhere." Sheriff Gooding twisted the handle and shined the light over the centerline of the cruiser's hood on two shadowy shapes up ahead.

"What in the world?" Mack cried out.

The light shined on the backsides of two giant blue tigers strolling nonchalantly down the middle of the street like they owned the place.

"They must have escaped from the circus," the sheriff said.

"I'll call Anna and let her know. She should still be there." Mack pulled his phone from his pocket and gave Anna a quick call. He told her where they were, that they had spotted two tigers, and after a few brief seconds ended the call.

"What'd she say?" the sheriff asked.

"She's going to find the trainer, Andrea. The tigers' names are Somba and Rumba."

"Well, that's good to know. Just in case we want to lure them with a treat."

"I don't think that's likely to happen," Mack said. "Anna said not to provoke them. Someone would be here soon."

"What about our suspect?" Sheriff Gooding said. "I can't just drive off and leave these two wandering the streets."

Mack saw a front door opening and a man come out of a house. A woman and a small girl were peering out the living room window. The man started down the walkway to his driveway to get a closer look at the pair of Maltese tigers sauntering by the front of his home.

"Will you look at that idiot," Mack said.

Sheriff Gooding grabbed the mike from his dashboard and clicked on the exterior speaker. "You outside! Get back in your house!"

The man turned and stared at the police cruiser. It was as though his feet were rooted to the ground and he could not make up his mind, which was more interesting, being addressed over a PA system by the town's sheriff or watching two jungle beasts waltzing down his street.

"Get moving you fool," Mack said though he knew the man couldn't hear him.

"I won't tell you again," the sheriff persisted on the loud speaker. "Get back in your—"

The larger tiger bounded across the sidewalk toward the curiosity seeker who was already trampling over his own flowerbed to scramble back inside his house.

Sheriff Gooding maneuvered the cruiser and blocked the other tiger. He blared the horn and turned on the high beams, blinding the big cat. It backed away and skulked off down the dark street.

The frightened man dashed inside his house and slammed the front door.

The tiger spotted the woman and child as they turned and ran back into the room. It leaped over a hedge and smashed through the pane glass window.

Mack jumped out of the car.

"Grab a shotgun from the trunk," the sheriff said, popping the release lever.

Mack went around to the back of the cruiser, reached in, and snatched a pump shotgun. He started for the house and heard the sheriff say, "I'm going after the other one," and the patrol car sped off down the street.

The front door was unlocked so Mack stepped inside and found the living room to be a shambles of smashed furniture covered with broken glass.

Mack heard the woman scream and a door slam.

He pumped a round in the shotgun's chamber and proceeded across the room. He looked down and noticed something strange. The stock and barrel of the shotgun were painted lime green.

Mack stepped around the corner and saw the tiger standing in the kitchen. It was staring through a glass door at the man, his wife, and child cowering in the back of the pantry.

Mack held his breath. The big cat hadn't sensed him yet.

Ropey drool hung from the tiger's lower jaw.

It was only a matter of seconds before the big cat burst through the flimsy door.

"Hey, over here," Mack said, taunting the animal.

The tiger turned and took a menacing step toward Mack leaving him no choice but to fire the shotgun.

Mack heard the projectile strike the tiger in the chest, then clatter on the floor.

"What the—" and then he realized what the green paint meant on the shotgun. It was loaded with beanbag bullets, which were painful but not lethal and were meant as a deterrent for crowd control.

The tiger growled.

Mack considered reaching for his sidearm with live ammunition but decided against it, afraid he might only wound the animal, making it more dangerous.

Instead he pumped the shotgun and fired again.

The tiger snarled when it was struck in the shoulder but moved back.

Mack glanced to his right. He was standing next to the refrigerator. He flung open the door.

Inside, on the middle shelf was a rump roast on a plate. He reached in and grabbed the big chunk of meat. "Chew on this!" Mack tossed the offering across the room so that it landed by the back door.

The tiger vaulted across the kitchen. It pounced on the roast with its rear end in the air and picked the meat up with its teeth.

Mack fired a beanbag bullet into the animal's testicles.

The tiger yowled, dropping the roast. The beast crashed through the back door and ran outside into the dark.

Mack went to the shattered doorframe and made sure the tiger was gone before telling the family they could come out of the pantry.

The man stepped out, followed by his wife and little girl.

"Everything's okay," Mack assured them. "It's gone."

"Thank you so much," the woman said.

"Yeah," the man said. "I guess that wasn't too smart going out there."

"At least you're all okay," Mack replied then turned when he heard heavy footsteps enter the house.

Sheriff Gooding raced into the kitchen with his gun drawn.

"It's okay, Sheriff," Mack said. "Our tiger's gone. What about yours?"

"It jumped over a fence and I lost it." The sheriff looked at the shotgun in Mack's hands. "Damn, I'm sorry. I didn't mean for you to grab that one," he laughed.

"Don't worry, Sheriff," Mack said with a smile. "It proved to be quite the ball buster."

44

WORK ORDER

Camden searched the neighborhood on his own looking for the van. Each time he spotted a suspect vehicle, he checked the registration sheet he had brought along with license plate numbers of the residents that lived in the gated community. So far, every van's license plate he encountered had been on the list.

He was infuriated with Sheriff Gooding for not taking him along in his cruiser to look for Suzie's kidnapper. Sure, Camden knew he was only a security guard and not a trained police officer but this was his daughter for god's sake.

He turned at a corner and rode up a steep street. He could feel the golf cart lug and knew the four batteries under the seat were in desperate need of charging. Not wanting to drain the batteries and end up on foot, he decided to go back down the hill and search the homes on flatter ground.

He glanced between two houses and saw a black horse without a rider leap gracefully over a wrought iron side fence separating two yards.

"What in the hell?" It had to be the same animal he had heard galloping by the guard shack. He knew it would be impossible to chase after the swift animal in the doddering golf cart and hoped it found its way back out so he wouldn't have to hassle with it.

He turned right onto Sagebrush Court, and as he was banking around the curved end of the street, he spotted an open garage.

Inside was a single vehicle.

A van.

Camden stopped the golf cart and looked down at the house number painted on the curb. It dawned on him that it was the same address on the repairman's work order to fix the garage door and the house was unoccupied.

He took his cell phone out of his pocket and was about to call the sheriff when his anger got the best of him. Inside that van was the monster that had abducted his daughter.

As he wasn't armed with a gun, he needed something to defend himself. He reached back in the small cargo space behind the seat and grabbed a crowbar.

Camden got off the golf cart and walked slowly up the driveway to the dark two-car garage. The first thing he noticed was the dented back doors of the van and realized the vehicle had been rear-ended.

He hefted the crowbar at his side, ready to swing at the first provocation, and stepped up to the driver side window. He peered inside the gloomy cab but there was no one there.

Camden crept back to the rear of the vehicle and pressed his ear against a door to see if he could hear anyone inside. He held his breath and listened. All he heard was his rapid heartbeat as the blood pulsed through his eardrum.

He stepped back, inserted the flat end of the crowbar between the two doors, and pulled back on the steel rod with all his might. The metal doors creaked so he kept trying to pry them apart. Suddenly they broke free. A door swung open almost striking Camden in the face.

He gazed inside and gasped, "Oh my God."

The crowbar slipped from his fingers and clanked on the concrete garage floor.

45

HOME INTRUDER

Sheriff Gooding insisted they warn the residents on the loud speaker and kept yelling into his mike for everyone to remain in their homes as he drove down the street.

Mack was growing impatient. "Sheriff, he's getting away."

"I'm sorry but I can't risk anyone getting hurt by those tigers."

"Then maybe—"

A car came around the corner, flashed its high beams, and skidded to a stop alongside the cruiser facing the opposite direction.

It was Anna. She lowered her window. "Andrea should be here soon with some trucks. Did you find our suspect?"

Mack leaned forward in his seat so he could see past the sheriff. "Not yet."

Sheriff Gooding's cell phone rang from the console mount. He reached down and picked it up. "Buckhorn Sheriff's Department." He listened for a moment.

"Who is it?" Mack asked anxiously.

The sheriff glanced over at the agent. "It's Camden. He found the van."

"Where?"

"All right. Someone will be right there," the sheriff said into the phone and ended the call. He looked at Mack. "It's four blocks down that way," he said, pointing back over his shoulder. "Sagebrush Court."

"What are you waiting for? Let's go," Mack shouted.

"You two go. I need to make sure those animals don't hurt anyone."

Mack jumped out of the cruiser and ran around to the other side of the rental car and got in beside Anna. "It's this way!" he yelled and pointed straight ahead.

Anna gunned the car before Mack could close the door.

They sped down between the houses.

Mack kept an eye on the street signs. When he spotted Sagebrush Court, he hollered, "Take a left here."

Anna circled the car around behind the golf cart and parked in front of the driveway leading up to the open garage door with the van inside.

They got out of the car.

Mack rushed over and peered inside the cargo hold. It looked somewhat the same as the last time he had seen it at the abandoned warehouse. The same vile mattress, crates full of clown and bondage paraphernalia, and other assorted junk.

"Where's Camden?" Anna asked.

"Right here," a voice replied from the corner of the garage.

Camden stepped out from the shadows with Suzie close at his side. Cindy Jacobs came out. She was wiping tears from her eyes.

Anna went up and put her arm around Cindy's shoulders. "You're safe now."

"Tell us what happened," Mack said.

"After I called the sheriff, I decided we should duck out of sight," Camden said. "Just in case that maniac came back for the girls."

"Good thinking," Anna said.

"After all the trouble he went through nabbing the girls, why did he just run off and leave them?" Mack asked.

"He tried getting to us," Cindy said. "But he couldn't open the doors. Mr. Fryer had to pry them open."

"You were both lucky," Anna said.

"Any idea where he might be?" Mack asked.

"No," Camden replied.

"Think he might have gone into the house?"

"It's possible," Camden said. "The home security system has been turned off so contractors can come in to do home repairs before the house goes back on the market."

"So the house is vacant?"

"That's right."

"I'm going in," Mack said.

"Not alone, you're not." Anna glanced over at Camden and Suzie. "Camden, why don't you take the girls down to the car. If you see anything, honk the horn."

"Will do." Camden escorted the girls down the driveway to the car.

The agents drew their service weapons.

Mack took out his penlight and shined it across the garage at the door leading into the house. He walked over, turned the knob, and pushed the door open. He glanced inside. "Looks like the kitchen. Stay frosty."

"Don't you mean, watch my six?" Anna said, standing behind her partner.

"Would you rather I said watch my—" but then Mack heard a noise and stopped his bantering. "He's in here." Not wanting to make himself a target standing behind the flashlight beam, he reached for the wall switch, and turned on the kitchen lights before stepping inside.

Mack crept around the counter island in the kitchen and moved toward the unfurnished family room. Drop cloths were spread on the floor next to a stepladder and a few cans of paint. "Careful," he whispered to Anna. "He could be hiding anywhere."

"Just let him pop his head up," Anna said, holding her gun in a two-handed grip.

They flicked on the recessed lights in the ceiling as they went. Each room was freshly painted.

Mack led the way down a hall. He stopped at what appeared to be the threshold to the master bedroom. The room was void of furniture like the rest of the house. Tarps were on the floor along with some paint cans.

The sliding glass door was standing open.

"He must have snuck out the back." Mack entered the room. He flicked on the wall switch but the overhead lights did not come on. He heard a rustling, and when he turned to the sound, he saw a dark shape move in the corner of the room.

"Anna, look out!" Mack yelled, and dove at his partner. He knocked her to the floor and ended up on top of her.

Mack heard a loud squawk.

A frightened bird launched itself off the top of a stepladder leaning against the wall. It fluttered about the room then flew out through the open doorway and disappeared into the night.

Mack gazed down at Anna. "Ah, sorry about that. Are you hurt?"

"Nah, not at all. I always enjoy a good tackling."

The car horn blared outside.

"They spotted him," Mack said. He jumped up and pulled Anna to her feet.

They raced back through the house to the garage.

46

ROUNDUP

"How does your head feel?" Keko asked, downshifting the semi truck as they entered the main entrance into Desert Sands Estates.

"Like a woodpecker is trying to get out," Andrea replied from the passenger side, her circus headache doing a tango with the painful lump on her head. She glanced in the side mirror and saw the two big trucks following behind driven by Bubba and Lou.

"That must be where they want us to go," Keko said, heading down the street toward the long row of flares. A police cruiser with flashing emergency lights blocked a side street. An ambulance was parked at the curb with its back doors open. Paramedics attended to two teenage girls while a middle-aged couple and a man stood close by watching and looked to be the concerned parents.

She saw Anna standing with her partner next to a four-door sedan.

The airbrakes hissed loudly as Keko brought the semi truck to a complete stop.

Andrea climbed out and lowered herself to the ground.

Bubba and Lou parked their trucks.

All three drivers got out and walked around to the back of the trailers loaded with the large cages covered with canvas tarps. They pulled down the ramps then opened the rear cage doors.

A campervan came down the street and stopped next to the trucks. The cab door opened and Rollo stepped out from behind the wheel. Magnus climbed out and rested his hand on the skinny man's shoulder.

The rear door of the camper burst open and the dwarfs spilled out like they were doing a routine. First came Half-Pint and Penny, then their son, Patches, followed by Dum-Dum, Slappy, and Duncan Doon. Pogo was the last one out. He was still dressed as the gnome statue and handler for the goblins.

Anna and her partner walked over to Andrea.

"This is Special Agent Mack Hunter," Anna said, making the introduction.

"Nice to meet you," Andrea said and smiled at Mack.

"How is Mr. Meyers doing?"

"It wasn't as bad as we thought. Our circus physician assured me Hank would be fine."

"That's good to hear."

"So what now?" Anna asked.

"Now, we try and round up those missing. That is if they're here."

"Well, we've seen the tigers," Mack said. "And the security guard says he saw a black horse jumping over fences."

"That would be Somba, Rumba, and the Kelpie," Andrea confirmed. "Did anyone see the gnomes?"

"If they did, no one reported it," Anna said. "We should try and make this fast. The State Troopers will be arriving soon to help us with our manhunt for the man that robbed your circus and kidnapped two girls. He's still around here somewhere."

"Yes, we better get started," Andrea said. "Do you have a bullhorn I could use?"

"No, but the sheriff has a public address system in his cruiser. Come on."

Andrea followed the two agents over to the cruiser.

"Sheriff Gooding," Anna said. "Can Andrea use your PA to call her tigers?"

"Sure." The sheriff reached in and pulled the mike from the dashboard. He handed the device to the woman. "Press the button to talk."

Andrea sat on the edge of the seat as the cord would only stretch so far. She depressed the button. "Somba! Rumba! Come here my pets!"

She kept repeating herself for almost a minute before someone yelled out, "I see them!"

Andrea handed the mike back to the sheriff and hurried over to the ramp where Keko was standing ready. She waved her arms as soon as she saw her tigers and beckoned them over.

Everyone gave the big cats a wide berth as they strolled shoulder to shoulder toward Andrea. "That's it my lovelies, this way." She swept her hand back along the edge of the ramp, directing her tigers to the cage entrance. Somba marched up the ramp first then Rumba paraded in.

Andrea waited until both Maltese tigers were situated and lying on the straw covered floor before shutting the cage door. She signaled for Keko to raise and store the ramp.

"It's your turn," Andrea said to Duncan Doon.

"Aye," replied the dwarf.

"What will he do?" Mack asked Andrea.

"Duncan is going to lure the Kelpie with a serenade."

"You can't be serious."

"If you don't believe me, just watch."

Duncan Doon scampered up to the top of the ramp. The dwarf raised his arms out by his sides like an opera singer on stage and sang in a sweet lilting voice:

My bonnie, my bonnie
Where can you be?
Out in the moors
Lost out at sea.
Wherever you are
Please come back to me,
Sweet Lola my dear
My lovely Kelpie.

A horse whinnied as soon as the last verse ended. Out of the darkness came an ebony mare. The magnificent beast galloped up the street. Its eyes glowed like two beacons on a dark stormy night.

Bubba stood by the ramp. The ex-boxer took a step back as the horse pounded up the ramp. The Kelpie stopped short of entering the enclosure. It lowered its head so Duncan could reach up and pet its cheek. "In you go, lass."

The horse let out a forceful snort and shook its mane then trotted into its cage.

Bubba jumped up and locked the door.

Andrea heard a scream and gazed down the street.

A cat raced down the tarmac like its tail was on fire. Three gnomes were in hot pursuit, gnashing their teeth. The feline darted under the sheriff's cruiser, eluding its pursuers.

Then a screaming teenage girl appeared with a young man running after her.

A small herd of goblins were right on their heels.

"Pogo, play your horn!" Andrea shouted.

Standing at the top of a ramp, the dwarf raised the alboka to his lips and blew out a long melodious tune.

The gnomes of Girona answered the call like the village rats marching after the Piped Piper of Hamlet and began hopping and scampering toward the bottom of the ramp.

Pogo continued to blow the horn until the last creature had gone up and was inside the cage. Lou jumped up to lock the door.

"Well, that was easy enough." Andrea said.

And then a scream pierced the night.

47

PIN THE TAIL

Anna drew her gun as soon as she heard the scream. It had come from behind the semi truck with the tigers aboard. She dashed around the front bumper and saw Elroy still wearing the hobo clown outfit holding Penny at gunpoint.

"Stay back," Elroy snarled at the FBI agent.

"Release her," Anna said. "There's nowhere for you to go." She motioned to the sheriff and Mack standing to her left with their guns drawn.

The dwarfs had congregated together on the sidewalk in a show of force.

Keko, Bubba, and Lou stood shoulder to shoulder like a trio of linesmen ready to rush the quarterback.

Andrea, Rollo, and Magnus waited anxiously by the camper.

The Fryers and Jacobs were too far away down by the ambulance to know what was going on.

Elroy yanked Penny up by the hair until she squealed.

"Let her go!" Half-Pint shouted.

"Don't you hurt my mom," Patches yelled, almost in tears.

Half-Pint started to rush the man holding his wife hostage. Dum-Dum and Slappy grabbed him by the shirt and yanked him back.

"Easy there HP," Dum-Dum said. "He's got a gun."

Elroy twisted a loop of Penny's hair in his fist and told her to keep still. He dropped the satchel of money on the runner under the cab door on the driver side. He reached up, opened the door, and tossed the bag inside.

"There's no point in running, Elroy," Mack said. "The State Troopers will be here any minute."

"Is that right. Back off, all of you, or I swear I'll put a bullet in her fat melon."

"Hey," Penny protested.

Anna spotted headlights coming down the street. "See, what did we tell you, they're here."

Elroy snuck a quick glance at the old-model pickup truck pulling up to the opposite curb. "Not in that heap they're not," he said and dragged Penny toward the cab door.

Andrea strode toward the trailer and shouted, "Somba! Rumba! Speak!"

The tigers' deafening roars billowed the canvas covering their cage.

It was enough to cause Elroy to jump back, and thus by doing so, he and Penny staggered across the sidewalk and ended up in front of a large tree.

Penny tried to break free but Elroy yanked her back.

"Let me go!" she yelled.

"Shut up you—" Elroy was shocked when he was struck in the right shoulder, the knife slicing through his coat and pinning him to the tree trunk.

"Keep yelling Penny!" Magnus shouted.

"He's right here," Penny screamed. "Over here!"

Magnus grabbed another knife from his belt and threw it. This time the blade hit Elroy's left arm and he dropped his gun.

The blind knife thrower snatched another knife and gave it a quick toss.

The blade missed Elroy's right cheek by mere inches.

Magnus reached for his next knife.

"Magnus, stop!" a woman's voice called out.

Anna turned and saw Lady McBeth and Tobias Morgan walking from the pickup truck. The right arm of the beautiful assistant was in a sling. She went up to her husband and placed her hand on his throwing arm. "It's over."

Half-Pint and Patches ran over to Penny as the other dwarfs cheered.

Sheriff Gooding and Mack placed John Paul Elroy into custody and handcuffed the suspect. They walked him down the street to the ambulance for medical attention.

Anna holstered her gun and was walking over to the rental car when she heard the big diesel engines start up. She turned and saw Rollo and the dwarfs piling into the campervan. Magnus and Lady McBeth were getting in the pickup with Tobias.

Before she could think to stop them, the vehicles had formed a caravan and were slowly heading down the street.

There was much that Mack and she needed for their report but it was nearly two o'clock in the morning and she knew everyone was exhausted.

She decided it could wait until tomorrow.
It had been one hellacious night and it was finally over.

48

LAST CALL

Kenny's truck churned up the gravel as he skidded to a halt in the Roadside Tavern parking lot.

He was rattled after seeing Ernie ripped apart back at the circus, and then fighting the insane traffic as everyone fled the fire. He still had no clue what had killed Ernie. All he knew was that he needed a stiff drink. He hoped no one inside remembered him leaving with Ernie. The last thing he wanted was a bunch of people asking questions about Ernie's whereabouts.

He got out of his truck and went inside the bar. As usual, the place was dark as a dungeon. The only illumination came from the two beer neon signs hanging on the wall behind the bar.

The bartender was slumped over the washbasin rinsing out some glass steins. He looked up as Kenny came in. "Not you again. Buddy we're closing up."

"Give me a quick shot." Kenny rummaged in his pocket and came up with a single bill.

Drying his hands, the bartender studied Kenny. "Jesus, you look like shit."

"You don't know the half of it. Give me a whiskey."

The bartender grabbed a bottle from the shelf. He filled a shot glass three-quarters to the rim, set it on the bar in front of Kenny then looked around the dimly lit establishment and shouted, "Last call!"

Kenny grabbed the shot glass and gulped the whiskey down. He glanced about to see what other diehards were still around. He recognized a couple of faces seated at the bar three stools down.

A lone trucker sat at a small table. Kenny had seen him on a few occasions.

Kenny gazed down the other end of the bar and saw a woman sitting by herself in the dark corner of the room.

"Who's she?" Kenny asked the bartender.

"Got me. She came in, sat down, and hasn't said a word. I gave her a glass of water figuring she'd drink it and leave. So far, she hasn't touched it. That was an hour ago."

"Maybe she'd like some company," Kenny said and got up from his stool.

"I wouldn't if I were you. Something ain't right."

Kenny ignored the bartender and sauntered down the bar. He scooted onto the bar stool next to the woman who seemed content to stare mindlessly at the liquor bottles on the far wall.

He leaned forward to get a look at her face.

"I know you," Kenny said.

It was the Filipino woman from the sideshow.

The neon signs flickered off and the interior of the bar suddenly went pitch dark.

"Hey, we get the hint," a man yelled. "Turn on the lights!"

"Quit your squawking, I didn't do anything," the bartender shouted.

The lights came back on for a few brief seconds; just enough time for Kenny to witness the beautiful woman transform into the hideous sideshow creature.

Able to see in the pitch dark, the Aswang grabbed Kenny and pinned his arms with its sharp claws. It leaned in and sank its teeth into Kenny's throat before he could even scream. The creature threw back its head with a mouthful of flesh, leaving a gaping wound in Kenny's neck that spurted blood all over the bar like a ruptured fire hydrant.

The two men at the bar slipped off their stools and fumbled their way in the dark for the front door. The Aswang jumped onto a man's back, and like a frenzied animal, munched on his neck until it severed the jugular vein.

Blood sprayed into the other man's face. "What the hell's going on here?"

The Aswang tackled him to the floor, and with three powerful swipes of its sharp claws, partially severed the man's head from his shoulders.

A flashlight came on and the beam shined on the blood-soaked creature.

"You're one ugly son of a bitch," the bartender said. He clicked back both hammers on his double-barrel sawed-off shotgun and fired.

The Aswang leaped to one side as the stunned trucker stood up from his table, squinting at the bright light. The barrage struck him in the chest and lifted him off his feet. He landed hard on the floor.

The bartender plucked the two empty cartridges out of the tubes and fed in fresh shells. He was closing the breech when the Aswang catapulted onto the bar.

"Son of a—" The creature leaped and knocked him to the floor slats behind the bar. The shotgun fired into the air blasting bottles to smithereens and splashing alcohol on the hot glass tubes of the neon lights. Flames erupted and spread like wildfire on the shelves. Then the bar top caught fire and the room quickly filled with smoke.

The front door flung open and a figure stood in the doorway.

"Belen!" J.J. Nightsinger shouted so as to be heard over the raging blaze.

The Filipino woman stepped through the swirling smoke, the intense inferno crackling around her. She went to Nightsinger and took his hand as though they were meeting on a clandestine rendezvous.

They turned their backs on the carnage and walked from the burning tavern.

49

SO LONG

Normally, Tobias would have been up an hour before dawn but as his tractor was broken down and he was exhausted from helping to combat the devastating tent fires into the early morning hours, he understandably overslept.

The walls of his bedroom rumbled suddenly waking him up. He slipped out of bed and padded barefoot to the window. He peered outside into the dark and saw the trucks passing between the barn and the farmhouse in a slow procession on their way to the main road.

Tobias threw on his overalls and boots. He dashed downstairs and rushed out onto his porch. He was surprised to see a congregation standing in the gloom at the base of the steps waiting for him.

"You're already leaving?" Tobias asked.

"Yes. Unfortunately it is best we go," J.J. Nightsinger said. "We didn't want to leave without saying goodbye and thanking you for letting us use your property."

"Anytime." Tobias cinched his overall straps over his shoulders and went to the head of the steps. The morning sun was beginning to crest on the far horizon providing enough light that Tobias could make out the faces looking up at him.

"So long, Mr. Morgan," Half-Pint said, his words echoed by Penny, Patches, Slappy, and Dum-Dum.

"Yeah, sorry about the mess," Penny said with a shrug.

"Uh, that's okay," Tobias said though he had no idea the extent of the damage to his land.

A horn honked and Tobias turned to see Rollo waving from his campervan, followed by Magnus and Lady McBeth in their motor home.

Keko and Andrea gave him a wave from their truck as the restless cats growled in the back.

Bubba and Duncan acknowledged Tobias as they transported the Kelpie snorting behind the closed tarp.

The gnomes chattered from their enclosure as Lou and Pogo passed by.

Samson was fast asleep in his cage as Armand drove behind the others.

"Well, we must be off," Nightsinger said. He walked over to his Cadillac convertible and got behind the wheel. Belen sat waiting in the passenger seat.

"Be seeing you," Half-Pint said as he and his family clambered aboard their motor home followed by Slappy and Dum-Dum.

Tobias watched them drive away. He turned and walked down the thoroughfare between the two buildings. He stood at the side door to the barn and saw a dozen or more abandoned cars and trucks. He could see the burnt remnants of the structures and collapsed tents. Once everyone claimed their vehicles and had them towed off his property, he would then worry about cleaning up the charred remains.

He opened the door and stepped inside the barn. Golden sunlight shined down from an open window.

Tobias heard something rustling under a mound of hay in a stall by the tractor. "Who's there?"

Two heads popped out of the dried fodder.

"Oh my Lord. What in the world are you doing here?"

It was the two humanoid Agogwe.

Tobias ran to the double doors and pushed them open hoping to flag down the departing circus. He was relieved to see Nightsinger's car idling by the side of the farmhouse. "I think you forgot something!" Tobias yelled.

"No, I don't think so," Nightsinger replied.

Anesu and Chindori scampered out of the hay leaving trails of straw. They jabbered like a couple of Teletubbies and scurried out of the barn where Nightsinger stood by the side of his car with the driver door open. The Agogwe climbed behind the tilted front seat and jumped in the back.

Nightsinger got in the car, and without further farewell, drove off.

Tobias turned and walked over to the tractor.

He spotted something on the seat and couldn't believe his eyes. Now he knew why the ringmaster had sent the Agogwe.

They had brought him the money he had been promised.

50

CLOSING THE CASE

It was late afternoon the next day and Anna and Mack thought they would drop by the sheriff's office to say goodbye before catching their flight back to the Bureau.

Joseph and Shelly were having coffee in the sheriff's office when they came in.

"Hi, there," the sheriff greeted when the two agents came to his door.

"We're just leaving for the airport," Mack said.

"How's that suspect of ours?" Shelly asked.

"We handed him over to the U.S. Marshals and they're escorting him back."

"He won't be giving us any more grief," Anna said.

"Well, that's a relief," Sheriff Gooding said.

The phone rang in the front office. Shelly excused herself to answer it.

"Care to give us a rundown before you email us your report?" Anna asked, stepping into the office. Mack came in and they stood by the credenza.

"Sure," the sheriff said and picked up a notepad off his desk. He gazed down at the first page. "We have one body found on the Morgan farm identified as Ernie Brown. Forty-seven people injured during the circus fire, three serious but none critical."

He flipped to the second page. "The same night our local bar burned to the ground. So far the Fire Marshall has recovered five bodies."

"How strange," Anna said.

Shelly stepped back into the room. "That was Vivian Campbell. She wants to come down and file a missing persons report on her husband, Bernard."

"When was the last time she saw him?" the sheriff asked.

"Last night before they went to bed."

"I see."

"That's not all. Seems another one of the residents of Desert Sands Estates has also gone missing. A Mark Taylor. He was supposed to meet with some friends but never showed up."

"You better keep us posted," Mack said.

"Sure," the sheriff replied. "As soon as I know something, I'll let you know."

"At least the girls are okay," Shelly said.

"That must be a big relief to both families," Anna said.

"Oh, yes."

"Any word on that circus?"

"Not since they left Tobias' farm," the sheriff said. "It's like they vanished into thin air."

Anna glanced at her watch. "We better go or we'll miss our flight."

The agents shook hands with the sheriff and his wife.

On their way to the car, Anna stopped to grab a newspaper from the vending machine on the sidewalk. Mack got behind the wheel and they headed out of town.

"Oh boy," Anna said after browsing the front page.

"What is it?" Mack asked, turning to follow the signs for the airport.

"Remember the Rollins family?"

"Sure. The senator running for president."

"Well, not anymore. He withdrew from the race."

"Why, he seemed like a good candidate."

"Turns out he was getting too much flack from the press," Anna said.

"Oh yeah? Why's that?"

"They've been calling him a raving loon for wanting to put microchips in every child in America."

"Really." Mack looked at Anna and grinned. "Wonder where he got that crazy idea?"

51

Found three months later posted on a tree in San Rio, Texas...

CRYPTID CIRCUS

THE MOST AMAZING SHOW IN THE WORLD
UNDER THE BIG TOP
UNIQUE ACTS AND INCREDIBLE CREATURES
THRILLS AND CHILLS FOR EVERYONE
CONSESSION STANDS AND GAME BOOTHS
AT THE HAMMER RANCH OFF HWY 4
PLENTY OF PARKING
COME ONE, COME ALL

TICKETS SOLD AT THE TICKET BOOTH

ACKNOWLEDGEMENTS

I would like to thank Gary Lucas and the wonderful people working with Severed Press that helped with this book. It's truly amazing how folks we may never meet and who live in the most incredible places in the world can collaborate and enrich our lives. Special thanks to Nichola Meaburn for catching my goofs and to my wonderful daughter and faithful beta reader, Genene Griffiths Ortiz for her enthusiasm, and making this so much fun. And of course, I would like to thank you, the reader, for taking the time to share these bizarre and incredible journeys with me.

ABOUT THE AUTHOR

Gerry Griffiths lives in San Jose, California, with his family and their four rescue dogs and a cat. He is a Horror Writers Association member and has over thirty published short stories in various anthologies and magazines, along with a collection entitled *Creatures*. He is also the author of *Silurid*, *The Beasts of Stoneclad Mountain*, *Death Crawlers, Deep in the Jungle*, *The Next World*, *Battleground Earth*, *Down From Beast Mountain*, *Terror Mountain*, *Cryptid Island (*prequel to *Cryptid Zoo)*, *Cryptid Zoo*, and *Cryptid Country (*sequel to *Cryptid Zoo)*.

CHECK OUT OTHER GREAT CRYPTID NOVELS

BIGFOOT WAR
by **Eric S. Brown**

Now a feature film from Origin Releasing. For the first time ever, all three core books of the Bigfoot War series have been collected into a single tome of Sasquatch Apocalypse horror. Remastered and reedited this book chronicles the original war between man and beast from the initial battles in Babblecreek through the apocalypse to the wastelands of a dark future world where Sasquatch reigns supreme and mankind struggles to survive. If you think you've experienced Bigfoot Horror before, think again. Bigfoot War sets the bar for the genre and will leave you praying that you never have to go into the woods again.

CRYPTID ZOO
by **Gerry Griffiths**

As a child, rare and unusual animals, especially cryptid creatures, always fascinated Carter Wilde.

Now that he's an eccentric billionaire and runs the largest conglomerate of high-tech companies all over the world, he can finally achieve his wildest dream of building the most incredible theme park ever conceived on the planet...CRYPTID ZOO.

Even though there have been apparent problems with the project, Wilde still decides to send some of his marketing employees and their families on a forced vacation to assess the theme park in preparation for Opening Day.

Nick Wells and his family are some of those chosen and are about to embark on what will become the most terror-filled weekend of their lives—praying they survive.

STEP RIGHT UP AND GET YOUR FREE PASS...

TO CRYPTID ZOO

CHECK OUT OTHER GREAT
CRYPTID NOVELS

SWAMP MONSTER MASSACRE
by **Hunter Shea**

The swamp belongs to them. Humans are only prey. Deep in the overgrown swamps of Florida, where humans rarely dare to enter, lives a race of creatures long thought to be only the stuff of legend. They walk upright but are stronger, taller and more brutal than any man. And when a small boat of tourists, held captive by a fleeing criminal, accidentally kills one of the swamp dwellers' young, the creatures are filled with a terrifyingly human emotion—a merciless lust for vengeance that will paint the trees red with blood.

TERROR MOUNTAIN
by **Gerry Griffiths**

When Marcus Pike inherits his grandfather's farm and moves his family out to the country, he has no idea there's an unholy terror running rampant about the mountainous farming community. Sheriff Avery Anderson has seen the heinous carnage and the mutilated bodies. He's also seen the giant footprints left in the snow—Bigfoot tracks. Meanwhile, Cole Wagner, and his wife, Kate, are prospecting their gold claim farther up the valley, unaware of the impending dangers lurking in the woods as an early winter storm sets in. Soon the snowy countryside will run red with blood on TERROR MOUNTAIN.

SEVERED**PRESS**

 facebook.com/severedpress
 twitter.com/severedpress

CHECK OUT OTHER GREAT CRYPTID NOVELS

RETURN TO DYATLOV PASS
by **J.H. Moncrieff**

In 1959, nine Russian students set off on a skiing expedition in the Ural Mountains. Their mutilated bodies were discovered weeks later. Their bizarre and unexplained deaths are one of the most enduring true mysteries of our time. Nearly sixty years later, podcast host Nat McPherson ventures into the same mountains with her team, determined to finally solve the mystery of the Dyatlov Pass incident. Her plans are thwarted on the first night, when two trackers from her group are brutally slaughtered. The team's guide, a superstitious man from a neighboring village, blames the killings on yetis, but no one believes him. As members of Nat's team die one by one, she must figure out if there's a murderer in their midst—or something even worse—before history repeats itself and her group becomes another casualty of the infamous Dead Mountain.

DOVER DEMON
by **Hunter Shea**

The Dover Demon is real...and it has returned. In 1977, Sam Brogna and his friends came upon a terrifying, alien creature on a deserted country road. What they witnessed was so bizarre, so chilling, they swore their silence. But their lives were changed forever. Decades later, the town of Dover has been hit by a massive blizzard. Sam's son, Nicky, is drawn to search for the infamous cryptid, only to disappear into the bowels of a secret underground lair. The Dover Demon is far deadlier than anyone could have believed. And there are many of them. Can Sam and his reunited friends rescue Nicky and battle a race of creatures so powerful, so sinister, that history itself has been shaped by their secretive presence?

Made in the USA
Middletown, DE
22 October 2021